Respectfully submitted
to Dwight and Helen

Dan

THAT MARRIAGE BED OF PROCRUSTES

and other stories

Daniel Curley, a native of East Bridgewater, Massachusetts, attended the University of Alabama. After working as a welder in New Orleans and Fore River shipyards during World War II, he taught English at Syracuse University and New York State Teachers College, Plattsburgh. He now teaches at the University of Illinois. He is married and has four children. Several of his short stories have been cited in Martha Foley's collection of *The Best Short Stories of the Year*. Mr. Curley is at work on a novel, *How Many Angels,* to be published by the Beacon Press.

THAT MARRIAGE BED OF PROCRUSTES

and other stories

Daniel Curley

BEACON PRESS   *Beacon Hill*   Boston

Copyright © 1957 by Daniel Curley

Copyright 1947, 1948, 1953, 1956 by *Accent;* copyright 1954, 1955 by Kenyon College; copyright 1955 by *perspective;* copyright 1952 by the Gargoyle Press, Inc.; copyright 1950 by Hearst Magazines, Inc.

Lines from "The Pasture" by Robert Frost are quoted by permission of Henry Holt & Company; lines from "The Snake" by D. H. Lawrence, by permission of the Viking Press; and lines by A. A. Milne, by permission of E. P. Dutton & Co.

Library of Congress catalog card number: 57-9950

Printed in the United States of America

Some of the stories in this collection were first published as follows:

"Saccovanzetti," in *Accent*, Summer 1948; "To Ask the Hard Question Is Easy," in *The Kenyon Review*, Autumn 1954; "A House Called Magnolia," in *The University of Kansas City Review*, Summer 1952; "The Appointed Hour," in *The Kenyon Review*, Autumn 1955; "The Score Keeps Changing," in *Accent*, Spring 1956; "The Bribe," in *Harper's Bazaar*, February 1950; "A Spring," in *New-Story*, November 1952; "The Ship," in *Accent*, Spring 1947; "The Night of the Two Wakes," in *Accent*, Summer 1953; "That Marriage Bed of Procrustes," in *perspective*, Autumn 1955.

"William Sanders and the Dream of the Future" and "The Fugitive" are here published for the first time.

Contents

To HELEN

Saccovanzetti

The council of war said, Today you'll have to be Saccovanzetti by yourself. We don't have enough in it for there to be two. So, Micky, you have to be Saccovanzetti and you have to hold up the factory and you have to be dead at the end. Remember you have to be dead. You can kill the paymaster but at the end you have to be dead.

It seemed to Micky that he always had to be dead. All his life he was always being dead. Nine years old—1927 minus 1918 gives nine—well almost nine, nine in October, and always dead. He looked down from the top of the sand pit across the glass-smooth pond where the cows stood knee deep in water and mud, up the long cool slope of the pasture and the old orchard, to the pine grove.

"OK," he said, "I'll be Saccovanzetti." He looked back at the group which had imperceptibly formed opposite him, drawing itself together and leaving him by himself. He looked away from the pond and pasture and wood and looked at the group—his brother Ed, Bobby Miller, and Don Conlin—and then he looked to his right at the level stretch of sand between him and the thicket that sloped down to the pond. He knew that after he killed the paymaster he would have to hide out in the thicket and try to outwit and outshoot those who could not be outwitted and outshot.

The loose sand near the entrance to the thicket was marked with signs of his death struggles of yesterday when he had been a German. The others liked to see him die because he died so well and so violently, because he seemed to put everything he had into dying, leaping into the air and falling or falling in his tracks without even putting out his hands (the sand was soft).

"OK," he said, "where will the shoe factory be?"

I

"In the basement of the old burned school," his brother Ed said. "Don will be the paymaster."

"Not me," Don said. "I don't want to be shot."

"Just for a minute," Ed said. "As soon as he starts his getaway you can be the one who calls the good guys, and then you can be one of the good guys who goes after him."

"OK," Don said, "but I don't see why I have to be shot all the time."

"Do you have a handkerchief to put over your face?" Ed said.

"No," Micky said.

"Give him your cowboy bandanna, Bobby," Ed said.

"Here," Bobby said, "don't lose it."

"Don't worry." Bobby, of course, should have been the bad guy: he had the bandanna. Micky began to tie the bandanna around his face. The policemen were getting into the police station —the same craterlike depression that had been the shellhole yesterday from which the doughboys had slaughtered the Germans as they came out of Belleau Wood. The paymaster was in his office counting money and glancing up every now and then apprehensively.

Saccovanzetti dropped over the edge of the sand pit and crept along the slope just below the top until he was sure he had between him and the paymaster a large bush growing inside the old foundation. Then he eased himself over the top and crawled toward the bush. The policemen watched him intently, but since no one had called them they could do nothing. As he rounded the bush the paymaster's head appeared over the old foundation. The paymaster was looking the other way. Saccovanzetti pushed his pistol forward and fired it an inch from the back of the paymaster's head. The paymaster yelled, whirled, and drew his pistol, firing twice.

"I got you," Saccovanzetti said. "Drop dead. You never knew what hit you." With extremely bad grace the paymaster sat on the ground. Saccovanzetti leaped into the office and began scooping up the money. He climbed out of the office and ran toward the thicket.

He could hear someone in the office frantically telephoning the police.

The police were streaming out of the police station as he ran past, but since they had first to go to the scene of the crime to investigate they had no way of knowing that he was the killer.

He sprang into the wide funnel-like opening to the thicket and took the path branching off to the right. He ran along the spine of the hill with the pond glimmering before him through the trees and the thin air of the cut-away hill on his right hand.

When he reached the place where the path dropped sharply down to the pond, he stopped and listened. He could hear nothing except the rasping of his breath and the pounding of a pulse in his throat. To get a better look back over the path he began to climb a small tree at the edge of the pit with its roots on one side reaching dryly down into sterile air. From a little way up the tree he could see Ed and Bobby and Don just running into the thicket. Without stopping they turned down the path he had taken. That was just luck—good for them, bad for him. There was no way they could tell he had come that way, for the sand everywhere was pocked with footmarks from one day to another.

Before he could get down from the tree he heard them running along the path, and before he could even think of flattening himself among the branches, they ran directly under him close together, straining forward like hounds on a scent. He held his pistol in readiness but he did not shoot although he could have shot all three of them like fish in a barrel: he was supposed to die, not they. He knew that if he started shooting they would groan and grimace and shoot him like a bird in a tree and he'd be dead. He wished that for once he could be a good guy so that when he got shot like a fish in a barrel he could get up clutching his shoulder or his side or his head, grimacing with pain, more dead than alive, but carrying on and eventually winning and, if there were girls in the game, having his head bathed and stroked in the hospital. When girls played there were always more wounded than killed outright, though sometimes the girls liked to have you die in the hospital so they could have a funeral for you.

He waited a minute. When he jumped down from the tree he dropped his gun, and as he was looking for it among the bushes he heard them coming back. He flattened on the ground not five feet from the path, his face pressed down so that it would not show white among the leaves.

"He must have gone the other way," Bobby said. They had stopped beside the tree.

"Maybe he's up this tree," Don said. He fired twice into the branches and stepped close to the trunk to look up.

Micky held his gun on Ed's head and waited, the taste of metal strong in his mouth and his sweaty body cold against the ground.

"Come on," Ed said. "We'll go back and take the other path. Let's not let him get too big of a start."

Micky rested his head on his arm and sank back against the ground, weak in the reaction. Then he got up and ran down the hill toward the pond. With one quick bound he was across the path that paralleled the pond about fifteen feet up the last precipitous slope. He sprang down to the narrow beach and huddled against the bank. He clutched his side for the pain of running and thought that he would be unable to move again and that he would have to meet them there by the pond and shoot it out hopelessly there with those who could not be killed. He waited.

Gradually the pain left his side, his pulse quieted, his breathing eased; and he knew that he could not stay there pinned against the bank. Sooner or later they would get around the corner of the pond and see him from the railroad embankment and pick him off sitting. He began to work along the edge of the pond away from the railroad. The narrow beach narrowed even further as he approached a point of land that jutted slightly into the pond.

The steep bank became steeper and dropped straight down into the water. Soon he was walking in the rapidly deepening water, and it was becoming increasingly obvious that he would never be able to reach the point. He stood in the water, his gun held high, and stared out over the pond. They passed on the path overhead while he flattened against the bank, hidden by the steep bank and the leaves. He tasted the dry metallic taste again, and his shirt clung cold to his back.

They went away. They had not yet thought of the pond. Sooner or later they would think of the pond. They would go all through the thicket and then they would think of the pond. He had to move.

The best thing to do would be to go on to the dam, climb down the dam to the river bed, and get clean away. That would be the best thing. But the pond was too deep and the bank was too steep; so there was nothing to do but go back and climb up to the path. He could follow the path to the other side of the point and then get down to the pond again.

He started back along the beach. He could hear them shouting in the thicket, and he realized that he would never get ten yards along the path.

Perhaps he could go in the other direction over the tracks. For a moment he looked at the nearby railroad embankment, but it was so high, so bare, so lonely that he knew he could never get across to the safety of the other side.

And then he found the raft. When he had gone down the beach before, he had walked right over it because it had been covered with branches. He had thought it was a tree fallen down into the water. But now when he needed it he found the raft.

He pushed the raft into the water. He found that it was level and dry only if he stood exactly in the center. If he moved or shifted his weight suddenly, the raft tipped and water sloshed across it. He worked cautiously up to the point, staying always as close as possible to the bank. Then he stopped poling and allowed the raft to drift almost imperceptibly until he could see around the point.

This he knew was the crucial moment. He had to get the raft in motion, and he had to steer its unwieldy bulk around the point. And just when he would most need his eyes to scan the bank for them, he would have to devote his entire attention to the raft. He gave a violent push with the pole. The raft jerked forward, tipping slightly. The water sloshed into his shoes.

Then he was in the wide open at the point. He felt for the bottom with his pole, but the water was too deep. He hung there like a duck on the water. He knelt down and paddled with his hands, glancing continually over his shoulder, expecting any minute to hear gunfire from the bank. Although the raft had seemed to hang motionless, he found, when he began trying to paddle, that it continued to drift farther from the shore. He paddled frantically. His arms ached with the effort, but at last the raft appeared to stand still.

If it had been difficult to check the motion of the raft, it was even more difficult to start it off in a new direction. His arms were too tired to keep up the sustained paddling needed to get under sluggish way. He sat on the edge of the raft and kicked with his feet—he was soaked to the waist anyway. When he turned to look at the bank, he saw that he was perceptibly closer. He felt with the pole for the bottom, found it, and pushed himself into the bank.

That had been luck, he thought, to get around the point without being seen. He sat for a minute in the middle of the raft holding onto a bush to keep from drifting away. When he was out there in the open, he had felt that if only he could get to the bank he would be safe, but now at the bank, he knew that he must keep moving down to the dam.

He stood up and started poling. It had been some time since he heard them. Perhaps they were up on top of the sand pit or by the railroad. He poled easily along and beached the raft beside the dam. He leaped from the raft to the bank. He sprang to the top of the narrow bank and for a moment saw the steep sliding path down to the groove of the river bed below the dam. For an instant he was poised gathering himself for the path down. From all sides deafening gunfire and close at hand. His heart stopped, his pulse exploded, and he fell to the ground.

"OK, Saccovanzetti," his brother Ed said, "get up. We filled you full of lead and now we're going to take you to Dedham for the trial."

"I'm going to be Judge Thayer," Bobby Miller said.

"No, I'm going to be Judge Thayer," Don Conlin said. "I had to be the paymaster and be shot. I got to have something good."

"You be Judge Thayer, Don," Ed said. "Bobby, you can be District Attorney Katzman. I'm going to be Governor Fuller, and President Lowell of Harvard and Attorney General Palmer."

"Aw," Don said, "what do you say? When you're those guys you always mess everything up."

In the distance a shrill whistle like a police whistle blew two long and one short. "They want us for supper," Ed said. "You're going to catch it, Micky, for getting your clothes soaked."

"I don't care," Micky said. He was sitting on the ground trying to catch his breath.

"You better care," Ed said.

"How come you found me?" Micky said.

"We were up on top of the sand pit and we saw the ripples out in the pond," Ed said.

"We figured it was you," Don said, "so we came down and followed you along the shore."

"I never saw you," Micky said. He stood up and they all started for home.

"We didn't see you either," Ed said. "We just followed the ripples."

"How come you tried to really get away?" Bobby said.

"You must be crazy," Don said. "Don't you know Saccovanzetti never gets away?"

They went on home, Micky knowing all the way that he would really catch it. When they went into the house Micky could smell the mingled supper smells. It seemed to him that there was a chocolate cake in there somewhere.

"Oh, Micky, Micky," his mother said, "what have you done now?"

"I fell in the pond when we were playing Saccovanzetti," he said. He looked at Ed, but Ed said nothing and went on up to their room.

"George, come here and look at this boy," his mother said.

He could hear his father getting up in the other room. The paper rustled loudly. His father came to the door, the paper held in his hand.

"Speak to him, George. Tell him he mustn't play that horrid game." His mother turned back to the stove.

"What now, son?" his father said.

"I was playing Saccovanzetti and I fell in the pond," Micky said.

"There's no need to tell him not to play that game any more, Grace," his father said. "They're going to the chair tonight."

"Yeah?" Micky said. His mother crossed herself quickly and went on with her left hand taking the chocolate cake out of the oven.

"This time for sure," his father said.

"Good," Micky said, "they had it coming."

"Don't be so bloodthirsty, son," his father said.

"You said so yourself," Micky said.

"I know," his father said. "But now we have more important business to attend to. A desperate criminal who has fallen into the pond and is wet and exhausted can't very well be sent to bed without supper, but he can and should be sent to bed directly after supper and without chocolate cake. Not only without chocolate cake tonight but also without chocolate cake as long as this cake shall last."

"Run now and get washed up," his mother said.

"You might as well get into your night clothes now," his father said.

Micky ran up the stairs. It hadn't been really bad. He was tired, much too tired to go out after supper. "Ed," he called. "Saccovanzetti are getting it tonight."

"Yeah?" Ed said. He was sitting on the toilet.

"Yeah," Micky said. "You're Saccovanzetti in the electric chair. I'm the warden and I'm going to throw the switch." He reached behind Ed and flushed the toilet. A look of frustrate rage blazed on Ed's face. Micky ran laughing to their room.

To Ask the Hard Question Is Easy

George and Alice Fuller had arrived, after fifteen years of marriage, at one of those periods that arrive at intervals to all—couples and individuals—of asking, What the hell is it all for? Instead of waiting like sensible people for the whole thing to blow over and amusing themselves in the meantime by making each other miserable, they decided to take time out and try to answer the hard question.

So George announced that he wouldn't teach in summer school. When he still refused after he was offered more money, his friends began to worry about him. Perhaps he was going to write a book? No, it wasn't that either. Research? No. Travel? No. By then his friends had run out of questions and abandoned him to his folly.

When Alice quit her job, the women in the office wanted to give her a baby shower, but when she wouldn't admit she was having a baby, they sulkily let her go as if she were somehow betraying the sisterhood.

Then they retired to a farmhouse in the Vermont hills. The farm had been in George's family from the beginning of things, and although he himself had never seen it, it had come down to him: the sagging house, the crumbling outbuildings, the wretched soil, the pastures filling up again with birch and pine. And the cold and never-failing spring. And everywhere the granite core of the mountain cropping out.

The house was inhabitable in summer. From time to time George had sold off timber enough to keep the house painted and the windows glazed and to have everything cleaned once a year or so.

The yard was ripe for haying when they got there, so they had it mowed, but after that, except for a daily trip to the village and a weekly trip to St. Johnsbury, they were alone as they had desired.

In going to the hills they were purposely cutting themselves off from the world. They took no books or records. They didn't have the *Times* sent. Their car radio had been broken for some time. They were stripping themselves down to themselves in an attempt to answer their question.

Alice began at once to hook a rug she really wanted to hook, not a scroll, a leaf, an opened rose as prescribed by her adult education teacher, but a Mondrian composition, stark and unshaded. And George, despite his denials, began to write a book—but really not quite a book or at least not a scholarly book, rather a sort of autobiographical novel with the working title The Life and Opinions of George Fuller, Gent.

George found that he liked the routine of country living centered around his work on the book. It filled his life completely yet it was strange enough to be satisfying at all times. It had its variations too, things that didn't come up very often but were so clearly a part of this kind of life that they were satisfactorily routine. Such a job was checking on the gravity-flow water system that led from the spring across two fields and under the narrow dirt road and on down to the house.

No doubt he would ultimately have to call the plumber to fix whatever was wrong, but he didn't want to have to endure again the tolerance of the man, who came from three towns away to scoop in one quick gesture a handful of leaves off the wire mesh that covered the end of the pipe in the icy spring. Leaves, now, George could handle—handle proudly, with savoir faire. Or if there should be a break in the pipe, he would like at least to be able to report wisely a break just where the pipe comes through the stone wall or about fifty paces down from the spring.

It was his intention to go check the water after lunch, but at lunch time the youngest son of their nearest neighbor drove over on a new tractor to pass the word that there was a telegram for them in the village. The telegram, it turned out, announced the immediate arrival of their dear friends Phil and Carol, who had been invited many times though never actually expected. There was now nothing for it but to leave at once for St. Johnsbury to meet the train.

"Well," George said, "I can always take him up to the spring with me when we get back, but I know what he'll say."

"How can you know what he'll say?" Alice said. "He's probably never seen a spring before."

"That doesn't matter. He'll quote Robert Frost:

> I'm going out to clean the pasture spring;
> I'll only stop to rake the leaves away
> (And wait to watch the water clear, I may)—"

"Yes," Alice said, "that's exactly what he'll say."

"Unless he can think of something more obscure," George said.

"No," Alice said, "in Vermont he won't be able to resist the Frost."

They were pleased with each other at that moment, more pleased than for a long time, and it seemed to George that the trip to Vermont was a very good idea indeed.

Still pleased, they met Carol and Phil in St. Johnsbury, and Carol was carrying The Book. Obviously she had been reading it coming up on the train and passing some of the choice bits on to Phil because they chuckled together about it all the way from the station up into the hills. George was too glad to see them though to have any sense of foreboding, but he was surprised that they should enjoy it so much. He himself had seen the rave reviews before he left the city and felt it was certainly one he could afford to skip. Possibly, however, he had been too willing to believe he could skip it: although he sometimes enjoyed that man's books, he always found his face insufferable.

He told Phil as much and they immediately became embroiled in the familiar discussion of the feasibility of separating the man from his art. They ran through it all with the conventional thrusts and parries: freedom and responsibility, truth and expediency, artist and citizen. They did Pound versus his Fascism and Céline versus his anti-Semitism. And Phil did a little specialty of his own on Dos Passos: the author of *USA* versus the writer for *Life*. George found it good to have the old arguments coming so easily to his tongue after a month of talking only of cows and fences and ice and kerosene and was both surprised and pleased to find that when you've been back in the hills a while even the oldest dialogue has new importance. Of course when they had said it all they both still thought what they thought.

George had got up early that morning and done his thousand words. Consequently he was free and expansive as they spread their blankets on the lawn for the sun ritual. He was so expansive that he even offered them Scotch in the middle of the day. It didn't strike him at all strange that Carol neither looked at him nor spoke to him when he gave her the drink: some of their most successful parties in the city would pass through stages when everyone was off in a corner with a book. So when Carol just reached around from behind her book, it was just like old times although old times were exactly what they had come to the hills to avoid.

"Carol," Phil said. "Carol."

"Hmm?" she said.

"It's about The Book," he said softly.

"Hmm, the book?" she said. "Oh, The Book."

"Do you remember what he said about the loneliness of Americans? Something about womb to tomb loneliness."

"I read it to you," she said.

"And something about everything in between being either standing around waiting for one or rushing around looking for the other." Carol grunted and began to settle back into The Book. "Well," Phil said, "did you notice the people waiting on the platform at St. Johnsbury?"

"No," Carol said, "I was much too busy meeting these wonderful people." She reached over and patted Alice's leg.

Alice didn't bite her hand or even look as if she wanted to, so George knew Carol must rate pretty high because if there was one thing Alice hated it was to be touched like that, particularly by women. "I saw the woman in the tailored slacks and the barefoot sandals," Alice said. "I couldn't take my eyes off those sandals. They must have cost a fortune. There was absolutely nothing to them."

"I saw them too," George said and let it go at that. He wasn't going to commit himself on the subject of barefoot sandals when Phil and Carol knew so much more than he did about Krafft-Ebing.

"She was part of it," Phil said. "At every station on the way up there were old men and young boys standing around, and there were people meeting trains and seeing people off, and there were people coming and going by themselves. And then when we began to get into the summer country, we began to see this woman on the platform. In Concord she was meeting a man, and in Woodsville she was meeting a woman. Did you notice who she met here?"

"Leave me alone," Carol said.

"OK," Phil said, "let's not spoil it for them."

"Nobody," Alice said. "I noticed particularly. She didn't really look as if she expected anyone, and when we left she was still there against the pillar, smoking with her long holder, staring directly through those drunk people who were making such a fuss about seeing that drunk man off."

"That completes the pattern," Phil said cryptically. "I wish I had remembered to notice."

George had remembered to notice but he knew very well that there are some things it doesn't pay a husband to admit noticing. When it was simply a question of noticing the sandals, he could admit that, but when it became a question of continued observation, that was another matter. "What's all this about patterns?" he said.

"The pattern of loneliness," Phil said. "Both of The Book and of life. Life imitating art. Loneliness made more horrible by the very nature of the ridiculous symbols of loneliness as arranged by The Book."

"Turn it off," Carol said. "Save it for your students. Wait until we've all read it."

"Yes," Phil said, "when we've all read it, we'll have a lot of new things to talk about and a lot of new symbols for old things. But there is one image that has been bothering me." Phil was always being bothered by images. "I can talk about this because you've already heard the basic idea mentioned, and this won't spoil it for you when you read it yourselves. It's about that womb to tomb loneliness concept."

"That again?" Carol said without looking up.

"I say," Phil said, "that the protagonist's first job in the lying-in hospital is absolutely ideal, of course, for anchoring that end of the concept in the concrete imagery of The Book. But the other end is left high and dry. Surely he could have found a better job for his hero at the end than a newspaper job. It doesn't fit except possibly as an intermediate step. But in that event the final step is missing. Aesthetically it's quite frustrating, especially in such a fine book, not to have the tomb adequately symbolized."

"Did he perhaps work in the newspaper morgue?" Alice said.

"Did he?" Phil said. And George was shocked for a moment to realize that Phil himself knew only the reviews and what Carol had read him.

"No," Carol said.

"Well—" Phil said.

"You had him worried a minute," Carol said.

"No," Phil said, "the newspaper wouldn't do at all."

"You're just picking," Carol said. "Now leave me alone."

"A slaughterhouse maybe," Alice said. It was easy to see that she was pretty well fed up with The Book, but even her husband ignored the signs because he liked to listen to Phil talk. It didn't matter what Phil talked about. Some of his best ideas—most interesting and useful to George—were tossed off in a subordinate clause anyway.

"That would be much too gross," Phil said.

"An abattoir?" Alice said, needling all of them because she was the only one who wasn't a Bostonian.

"I can't think of anything that wouldn't violate the objective level," George said.

"More Scotch," Alice said. Even George himself knew that he was about to spring on to one of his favorite hobbies and bore the hell out of everyone, and more than that he knew that Alice must have expected to be very badly bored because she usually held back on the Scotch.

Carol went into the house for more cigarettes, and when she came back Phil was reading The Book. She snatched it away from him. "You can be next," she said.

"Me next," George said.

"Then me," Alice said, "in self-defense. But right now, the water, George."

"Forgot all about it," George said.

"Why worry about water when the Scotch is flowing?" Phil said.

"Basic stuff," Alice said, "like cooking and flushing the john."

"You can't use Scotch for that, I guarantee," Phil said standing up. "What do we have to do about water? Use a dowsing rod?"

"Oh, we know where the water is all right," Alice said. "The problem is why it isn't getting into the house."

"The pipe may be broken or clogged at the spring," George said wisely. "I'll have to go take a look. Feel like a little walk?"

"Fine idea," Phil said. He assumed a formal attitude for declamation:

> "I met a man as I went walking;
> We got talking,
> Man and I.
> 'Where are you going this nice fine day?'
> (I said to the man as he went by).
> 'I'm going out to clean the pasture spring;
> I'll only stop to rake the leaves away
> (And wait to watch the water clear, I may)—'
> 'I'll come with you, Man,' said I."

Phil sipped his drink modestly. "My humble apologies to A. A. Milne and Robert Frost," he said. "Bless them both."

George and Alice exchanged a look of triumph, but George wasn't sure it was the same triumph. They had both called the Frost perfectly, but George himself was delighted that Phil had surprised him with a variation.

"How about it, girls?" Phil said. "Or aren't you the water-seeking type?"

"Not me," Carol said without looking up.

"I'll stay with her," Alice said. She stretched out on the blanket and closed her eyes.

"I want to finish The Book," Carol said.

"That's fine," Phil said. "I'll be glad when we've all read it, so we can really talk about it." Both Alice and Carol seemed unconscious of their going.

By the time they had gone a hundred yards, the mountain began to tower between them and the sky, and they instinctively turned toward the house, which was now so far below them they could see over it and across a small valley to the next farm and then down along that valley into the great Connecticut Valley and the misty distances of New Hampshire. Off near the edge of the world, bursts of reflected sunlight came and went—perhaps cars on a highway—and a single large dazzle—perhaps a new barn roof—hung in the sky. On a hill near at hand a premature airline beacon turned and turned and turned its one pale eye upon them.

"In the morning," George said—"sometimes until quite late," he said by way of apology for knowing about the morning—"in the morning the whole valley is filled with mist. Here we sit up above it, looking down on a smooth white sea. It's eerie. You get a feeling that something has happened down there. A flood perhaps. Like the old woman and old man who entertained a god and were saved when all their wicked neighbors were drowned."

"Philemon and Baucis," Phil said.

"There used to be a world there. And poof, gone."

"You're getting to be quite the nature boy," Phil said. He hesitated a moment. Then he said:

> "Where are your books? that light bequeathed
> To Beings else forlorn and blind!
> Up! Up! and drink the spirit breathed
> From dead men to their kind."

"Books," George said automatically.

> "Books! tis a dull and endless strife:
> Come, hear the woodland linnit,
> How sweet his music! on my life,
> There's more of music in it."

"Of course you don't believe that?" Phil said.

"Of course not," George said, a good bit too quickly. "I just couldn't resist it. I don't get many chances to catch you off base, forgetting the poet's own reply."

"I didn't forget it," Phil said. "I just hoped I could get away once with quoting out of context."

"Your sins have found you out," George said. "Look out for the barbed wire." He lifted a strand of wire along the stone wall so that Phil could climb through. He felt a momentary blankness at the blank expression that passed across Phil's face. "Oh," he said, "you thought it was a quotation you couldn't place."

"A paraphrase," Phil said. "I thought you were paraphrasing something that ought to be something like: Your sins have found you out/Look out for hell fire."

In the middle of the next field George stopped. "Here's the spring," he said, looking down into a small pool of clear water.

"It's not exactly what I expected," Phil said. "I thought it would be more like a bubbler."

"Look way down," George said. "You can see the sand boiling."

Phil knelt on a rock in the attitude of Psyche at the spring and peered into the water. "Yes," he said, "I see it. What's the pipe?"

"The intake for our water supply. The leaves over the end of the pipe are the trouble we came up to take care of. Clean them off, will you?"

Phil dipped his hand into the water. "My god, it's cold," he said. Then he rolled up his sleeve and reached again. Then he took off his shirt and plunged up to his shoulder and at last reached the leaves. As his face lay just on the surface of the water, a small green snake swam away and disappeared between the rocks that defined the further limit of the pool.

Phil jerked his arm out of the water. George laughed. "It was a snake," Phil said. "He almost touched me."

"He was harmless."

"But a snake in the drinking water. How can I drink any more of it?"

"The old timers said that if snakes and frogs live in it that's a sure sign it won't kill you," George said.

"Old wives' tale," Phil said, still visibly agitated.

"Remember what Lawrence said after he repented chasing the snake away from his fountain:

> I missed my chance with one of the lords
> Of life.
> And I have something to expiate—"

George stopped for he suddenly foresaw the next and final line of the poem: *A pettiness.* He flushed. Now he had been badly guilty himself of lifting from context.

But Phil said, "I don't know the poem. Lawrence, you say? You didn't just make it up?"

"It's called The Snake or perhaps just Snake. Snake, I think."

The trip back down the mountain was quicker because instead of going through the fields they followed the road, a tunnel of green lightly silvered with dust. They stopped in the house for fresh drinks and went out to lie in the sun, which then seemed to be resting on top of the mountain.

"The water should be OK now," George said.

"It is," Alice said. "I was drawing water to heat for supper when it came with a rush."

"Let me help with supper," Phil said, lying down and closing his eyes. "I'll make my special scrambled eggs. We've been drinking Scotch so long now that it feels like breakfast time."

"OK," Alice said, "in about fifteen minutes or so."

Carol was still reading The Book, and they left her laughing on the lawn when they went to get supper.

Phil made a big production of the eggs because he was by now really feeling his liquor. He hovered over the skillet saying, Garlic, and George and Alice would say, Garlic, and slap it into his hand the way doctors do in the movies. Worcestershire. Worcestershire.

They laughed hilariously, but then they had drunk a lot of Scotch before supper.

Carol came in just as Phil dished up the eggs. "I've finished it," she said. Phil took The Book and sat down at the table and began to grope around for his food. Carol buttered his bread for him and gave him eggs and slices of the Spam that Alice had thoughtfully cooked on the side, knowing that even one-dish cooks can't stand a one-dish supper no matter how much Scotch they've drunk.

"This is priceless," Phil said beaming all over the rest of them. "Priceless. That part where he is interviewing the visiting English author."

"You mean," Alice said, "where the English author talks about the overheated American houses and the American matriarchy and the American women, standardized and deprived of sex?"

"Have you read it?" Carol shrieked.

"Do I need to?" Alice said.

"Not if you have a nasty enough mind," George said.

"Phil," Carol said, "isn't that just it? About The Book, I mean. He has a wonderfully nasty mind, hasn't he?"

"In the *Tribune* he looked like a eunuch," George said.

"The man versus his art," Phil said from behind The Book, only it didn't sound so good this time because they had been all over that once and the Scotch was beginning to wear off.

After supper Phil and Carol went off for a walk in what was left of the twilight. George fell heir to The Book and churlishly abandoned Alice to the dishes so that he could get in some good uninterrupted reading. Before long he came to the interview with the English author. He had to admit it was amusing but when you come right down to it, it was only what Henry Miller, among others, had been saying for years. And then there was that already famous passage in which the hero tries to seduce the girl by reading her passages from various novels and pathetically delivering a lecture on love in the 20th Century novel. Although neither Phil nor Carol had mentioned this part of The Book, George thought it particularly well done and most expressive of the central theme of loneliness: the quintessential point at which the hero wants to seduce the girl yet is so afraid that she will understand what he is about that he subtilizes his every chance out of existence. George had to go out and read that part to Alice.

"Does the girl understand?" Alice said.

"Yes," George said. "It's rather like Henry James."

"What does she do?" Alice said.

"She can't bring herself to go through with it on those terms. Somewhat Joycean."

"Does he know that she knows?"

"Yes, but he has said it in the only way possible to him."

"Oh," Alice said.

"Doesn't it begin to sound a little like Kafka?" George said.

"It doesn't sound very funny," Alice said.

"As it's written it is," George said.

"No, not really. Only at first. There's a kind of inward after-bite." George could see that she was beginning to brood, and since she wasn't at her best when she brooded, he tried to bring her out of it by reading some of the interview on the standardized female.

"You and your standardization," she said. "But aren't you afraid of spoiling it for me?"

"I didn't say I believed it," George said. "I only said it was amusing."

"Ha, ha," she said and went on with her dishes. George cursed himself for bringing it up at all.

When Phil and Carol came back, George was reading by a kerosene lamp and Alice was working on her hooked rug. "How appropriate," Phil said.

"What's appropriate?" Alice said because George wouldn't answer.

"That he should be reading The Book by the light of a lamp in which a moth is being cremated."

George looked up and saw a thick streak of soot on the lamp chimney. "I thought I was going blind," he said.

"What's so appropriate about that?" Alice said, jabbing viciously at the rug.

"The Book—" Phil and Carol and George said. They stopped and looked at each other laughing.

Then Carol said, "The Book is about a man who destroys himself seeking light." Alice jabbed on without comment.

Carol stopped for a moment beside Alice's rug frame. "I love your rug, Alice," she said.

"It's beginning to bore me," Alice said, "but I'm determined to finish it anyway."

"Oh, no," Carol said, "it's handsome."

"Handsome," George said.

As he was sitting down Phil said, "Have you noticed the girl's name yet?"

"Yes," George said, which was no lie, although he knew very well that what Phil really meant was if he had noticed the peculiar significance of the girl's name. It had seemed to him an ordinary name.

"Olivia Morsby," Carol said significantly.

"Yes," George said, "I noticed that." Rightly or wrongly it had suggested a town in Australia.

"But did you notice how many times the name is reversed as in roll calls, duty rosters, subscription lists?"

"As in Morsby, Olivia?" George said.

"As in Morsby, O," Phil said.

"It's all Greek to me," George said.

Phil smiled. "Not quite," he said. "*Bio* is indeed from the Greek, meaning *life*, but *mors* is from the Latin, meaning *death*. A subtle fusion of life and death and a subtle confusion of languages suggesting the confusion of the character and her ambiguity for the story."

"Then that explains," George said, suddenly seeing the light, "the significance of the hero's calling her Morsby until he becomes infatuated and after that calling her Olivia, suggesting olive, suggesting life."

"Exactly," Phil said.

"Deluded fool," Carol said.

"My sacroiliac," Alice said, "from the bottom of my back, suggesting pain."

"Now, now," George said. It was rather quiet after that, and George finished The Book easily. Phil took The Book with him when he and Carol went upstairs.

When Alice and George were in bed, he put his mouth against her ear and said, "I didn't think it was so hot."

"Well," Alice whispered, "look who's getting professional jealousy. He sits at a desk for a few hours for a few days pretending to write a novel and he feels he's entitled to professional jealousy."

George recoiled and was silent. He had been excited by the liquor and the conversation. He had remembered—out of the whole day—the moment of closeness just after the telegram arrived and then later that moment when Phil actually used the quotation they had predicted. Out of the whole day he had remembered those two things and forgotten everything else, and out of fifteen years he had forgotten everything.

"Now he's an author, he thinks. Well, what I think is he's still the same old stupid George Fuller the man who could have been chairman of the department and maybe president of the college if he just wasn't so stupid and wasn't always lousing up everything I try to do to cover up how stupid he really is so no one will find it out but oh no he's too stupid all the time to be covered up for and men who aren't one two three to him get ahead of him even when I beg and plead and cry and scream George I say that guy is dangerous so watch out for him but does he listen not George he's too stupid and besides everybody is his friend and wouldn't do anything like what I'm always thinking with my nasty mind about people like Matthews who was out to get him from the first day he came on campus the way he worked it so that one by one we had no friends left so one by one we couldn't go to this house or that house because the one person he had to get along with he was too stupid to get along with that Matthews who took over our friends one by one and who was it but old George who couldn't believe a person could really be like that until it was too late to save even one friend to keep me from being lonely all the time and he has to read about loneliness in books because he can understand only what's in books except that he's too stupid to really understand what's right there even in his books if he could only see it the way he can see an empty glass and fill it up with seven dollar a bottle Scotch as if it was water to wash in or flush the john with the way that half-baked Phil wanted to do before he got so drunk on it that he didn't want to do anything but pinch me in the kitchen with my lord and protector standing right there laughing and laughing and passing him the garlic so he can make his eggs with one hand and pinch me with the other good old Phil our real old buddy Phil who wouldn't know a man from an art if they both hit him at once and can only quote books while my stupid husband oh's and ah's about how clever he is and laughs at his jokes but never at mine and says what was that again Phil whenever Phil says some stupid thing that ought not to be said even once but when I say the sandals must have cost a fortune there was nothing to them my husband doesn't want to hear it once let alone twice. . . ."

It had no edges. It never had. Nothing to get a hold of or attack. But George knew that silence would only infuriate her further and that she would start to scream if he didn't say something. "You offered them Scotch yourself," he said, wishing Phil and Carol had never been born.

"Now he wants to argue. Whatever will he be wanting next? Well, let me tell you something. If I hadn't offered them Scotch you would have bored them to death and they are the only people left who are still speaking to us and I'd have been completely alone as if I could ever be more completely alone than I have been since I married him the selfish stupid bastard who I can never count on for a minute never feel a minute's security without wondering what stupidity he'll commit next and how he'll louse up something else we ought to have no matter what little or big whether it's a coupon for soap flakes he's too good to use or a full professorship he kicks out the window because he thinks somebody really wants to know what he really thinks about that somebody's book as if what a stupid bastard thinks matters about that or even about that girl in New Orleans. . . ."

"My god," George said, "that was on our honeymoon."

"Even on his honeymoon he is stupid. Even on my honeymoon I am alone. And let me tell you it's better to have a nasty mind than no mind of your own at all. If you didn't think it was so hot, why didn't you tell them so, them and their insufferable book?"

"Host-guest," George whispered, using as few words as possible, hoping to precipitate as few as possible.

"Try being a host unto me," Alice said, and George could tell she was pleased with that remark, so he went to sleep.

They had a late breakfast the next day, and it all started off beautifully, like the first morning of the world. But then Phil had to ask, "Did you notice the name of the paper he worked for?"

"The *Agora*?" George said. "That's Greek too. I know that from psychology, *agoraphobia*, the fear of open places."

"Right," Phil said. "Of course you know that *agora* by itself means *market place*, hence, on the objective level of the story, its appropriateness as the name of a paper. But still I think you are right in making the association agoraphobia. Did you notice how often he is alone in the office of the paper, in the deserted warehouse? And do you remember when he is crossing the field how the paper blows up against him, frightening him half to death? That paper was the *Agora* too. The very paper he works for."

"Yes," George said. "Yes."

"Well," Alice said, "let me tell you. The man is a jerk. Anyone who tries to write about an advice to the lovelorn editor after *Miss Lonelyhearts* is a jerk."

"You have so read it," Carol said.

"Of course," Alice said. "I took it out of your room after you were asleep."

"You were in our room while we were asleep?" Phil said.

"I just took The Book," Alice said. "I didn't suck any blood." She reached the pot off the stove and poured everyone a second cup of coffee.

So they had all read The Book, but somehow they never did talk about it although Carol and Phil didn't leave until Wednesday. It was just as well that the Scotch was broken out in honor of their going because there was a long wait at the station. As it was, the time passed hilariously. The old men and the boys stared at them with customary hard-faced curiosity, and the summer people ignored them. Despite the wait, the final farewells were so hurried that George barely had time to shake hands with Phil and Carol, and the kiss that Carol aimed at Alice somehow missed.

As much as George and Alice missed Phil and Carol, they found it good to be alone again and to sink back into the routine of life centered around George's work on his book and the homely necessities of life on the mountain.

One of the necessities that George had to face, and that within a few days of the guests' departure, was digging a new garbage pit. He intended to make it a fine deep pit, one that would last all summer, so after lunch he said goodbye to Alice at the kitchen door as if he were going off to the distant mines and shouldered his shovel and crossed a hundred yards of field to the spot he had selected near an old lilac bush growing at the edge of a shallow depression that might perhaps represent an old cellar hole. He glanced at the house but Alice wasn't in sight, and then he began to dig tentatively as a man will when he isn't used to digging and isn't sure how tough sod is and what is the weight of a shovelful of dirt.

Before he had been shoveling five minutes he could feel the sweat starting on the crown of his head. By the time he had cut the outline of the hole—five by two, and he hoped to dig about five deep—he felt the great drops of sweat standing on his forehead and in his eyebrows. He didn't wipe the sweat away: it was honest. He felt honest with the sweat standing on his face. But he knew Alice wouldn't like the sweat if she saw it. "Wipe your face," she would say. "It makes me hot to see you perspire so." He stopped digging long enough to brush the hair out of his eyes with the back of his hand. When he had done it he knew he must have left a streak of dirt on his face. Well, dirt was honest too.

As he dug himself deeper and deeper into the garbage pit that would last all summer, he watched Alice hanging out a wash. He watched her without stopping in his work, but once he did stop and lean on his shovel to watch the cows being driven to the barn at the nearest farm across the valley. The cries of the farm boys were faint on the light breeze as they worried the toy cows toward the toy barn.

He wiped his arm across his forehead, and he rubbed his hands on the legs of his new dungarees, and he spat into the fresh-turned earth beside the hole. All this was honest, a part of the feeling of honesty growing out of the work, real work with real things. Although he was completely out of condition he worked steadily on with the sweat running down his back and down his legs, with the blisters forming and breaking on his hands. The pain too was honest.

He would have to tell Alice that already he had a new sense of power, that he felt younger, stronger, more clear-eyed despite the sweat which frequently blinded him. He looked toward the house.

He was conscious of a tensing of his facial muscles as he saw his wife. She had changed into a halter and slacks, and although he was too far away to see clearly, he knew the outfit well. The halter showed the ugly roll of fat that came out from under her arms and extended across her back, and the blue slacks—doubtless without a girdle—certainly didn't flatter her and reminded him of time's implacable passing, which he felt he could forget without such an object lesson constantly before him. He saw her passing from the house to the clothes yard, and he could imagine the tiny drops of perspiration shining in her mustache, which had been growing so pronounced in recent years.

Once she looked up the hill and waved to him. He brandished the shovel over his head in reply. She disappeared into the house, and he again attacked the earth. He didn't see her for some time, and he felt again the strength and youth he had felt at the beginning. When he couldn't see her he confused her with his own feeling and thought of her as young and beautiful. He wanted to run to the house to tell her that he had now found what they had come to the hills to find: a new hope, a new life.

He felt now that everything could be saved and all questions answered. He relaxed for a moment and with careful strokes of the shovel trimmed the sides of the already trim hole. The firm earth held the marks of the shovel the way an old beam holds the marks of the adze. It was indeed an honest hole, a hand-hewn hole of which he could well be proud. It looked like a smallish grave.

He heard the tuneless singing of his wife in the house, and he savagely kicked the blade of the shovel into the earth at the bottom of the pit. The shovel hit stone and the shock passed all through his body leaving his leg numb to the hip. He felt cautiously with the shovel for the edges of the stone, but he could find no edge, so he began to scrape away the loose dirt. On top of the hard stone there was an inch of rotted stone. He dug easily through that and came to the solid core of the hill itself.

The pit wasn't quite so deep as he had planned, but it would do. He could burn it every once in a while so it wouldn't fill up so fast.

"Come up and see your garbage pit," he called toward the house.

"Coming," Alice called.

He could tell by her voice that she was humoring him in his quaint pride in one of his projects. He waited tensely in the hole, squaring the square corners and trimming the trim sides, scraping the stone until it was white with its own dust. It would really make an excellent grave. But he couldn't do it. Probably lots of people could but he couldn't.

He heard her coming through the grass, but he kept on with his busy work. When she stood beside the hole, he straightened. "A very good pit," he said.

"Yes," she said, "a very good pit. Not quite so big as I expected but it will do nicely. Pass me the shovel and come out for supper."

He passed her the shovel and braced himself to spring out of the hole. "I could eat a horse," he said.

"It looks like a grave," she said.

Quickly he lifted his face toward her. Could she? The thought burst upon him. She was standing over him with the shovel held like an axe. Her face was expressionless. The beads of perspiration gleamed on her upper lip. Yes, he thought, she could.

But she didn't. Instead she tossed the shovel aside and reached down to give him a hand. "Come on," she said. "I baked you a pie." He was deeply moved, but whether because she had baked him a pie or because she hadn't bashed in his head he couldn't say.

In his study after supper George sat at his desk in the attitude that Alice respected as the attitude of work. He smiled to himself when he heard her singing as she did the dishes, and he laughed as he watched her go across the field with a pan of garbage for the new pit.

His work didn't advance that evening because he got side-tracked and did nothing but contemplate the image of marriage as two people facing each other across a hole in the ground that might become a grave or a garbage pit. Even that episode at the pit then had been a part of the routine representing the particular tolerances and forbearances that constituted the equilibrium of their particular marriage. But he didn't quite see how that helped to answer their question. He wrote it all down though and set the manuscript aside to be thought about sometime.

Shortly after that Alice finished her rug, but she was disappointed in it. So was George for that matter although he gallantly spread it on the floor beside his desk. He himself was getting bogged down for lack of adequate library facilities—he often found it impossible to know the opinions of George Fuller (Gent) without the proper reference books—so about two weeks after Phil and Carol left, George filled in the garbage pit, that tiny hole in the mountain's side, so it wouldn't be a danger to anyone crossing his land. Then he shut off the water and closed up the house. The Book, which had been forgotten by Phil and Carol, was left on the night stand in the guest room, and since George hasn't had a summer off since that year, it is probably still there unless the cleaning woman did with it whatever it is that cleaning women do with things.

A House Called Magnolia

That time my mother came down to see me graduate and to see the place I had known so well and so long was an anxious time for both of us. I felt that I had a lot to say to her just then, and I think she felt it too because she gave me every opportunity to say what I had to say in my own way.

The best way I could think of was to take her on a big swing down through the country I knew as I knew no other country, not even the country she and I had known together. The rent of the car alone was going to run me at least ten dollars that I was going to need in New York while I was getting started, but I was glad to spend the money because I had to show her something. I didn't know then exactly what it was, and I still don't know, but I thought I could show it even if I couldn't say it.

I can't say I succeeded because all day I had the feeling that whatever it was I was trying to say wasn't coming through. The magnolias were just gone by, and the cotton wasn't very far along yet, and I had soon discovered that there wasn't very much I could show my mother about dairy farms. Even the cardinal I pointed out my mother remembered having seen once on a bird walk with her eighth grade class at home. She had, however, never seen two buzzards flop grudgingly off the carcass of a dog. That made an impression on her. I thought for a moment she was going to be sick. But we drove on rapidly and soon it was all cotton again. All day I was increasingly glad that I had saved Magnolia until the last.

It was well into the evening when I turned off the highway onto the long rutted drive that led up to Magnolia, greatest of all the plantation houses left in that part of the state. We followed the winding pitted drive around the weed-choked pond and came out from behind a clump of trees. With great banners of sunset behind it, Magnolia stood at the top of the rise at the end of the road.

"Lovely," my mother said. I stopped the car and we simply sat and looked. She was clearly impressed again, and this time impressed in a way she had anticipated in the morning as we started out. Then she said, "Shall we go closer?"

"I suppose so," I said. As we drove closer and entered the shadow of the house, I could hear my mother suck in her breath sharply and let it out slowly like a low soft sigh.

During the day I had once stopped to pretend to look at a tire while my mother got a good look at a shack close to the road. The shack was warped and weathered. It was a terrible gray. Windows broken. Boards hanging loose. Steps sagging.

And so was Magnolia.

However, we got out of the car. I had come too far now not to make an attempt to show this house which I knew was certainly everything that had made my mother gasp twice. As we stepped up on the porch, a tall thin man in sun tans came around from the side of the house and entered the porch from the end. He walked lightly and noiselessly toward us. When he got closer I saw that he was wearing broken tennis shoes. His hair was salt and pepper, and his face was browned and cracked into that expression that serves Southern males for the greater part of their adult lives. "Welcome to Magnolia," he said.

I didn't know what to say. "It was breathtaking," my mother said, "as we came up the drive."

"In all my life," the man said, "it has never let me down. If I have just walked down to the pond and right back, that first view is always the same."

"Magnificent," my mother said.

"By your accent you are not from this part of the country," he said. "But I seem to have seen you before, sir."

"Yes," I said. I swallowed hard. I hadn't realized how much I wanted him to remember. "I've been here a number of times with Judge Wilder."

"Of course," he said. "Will you come in while the light holds?"

"I live in his house," I said.

"Yes," he said. "It comes back to me now. We have missed him of late."

"He doesn't get around much since his accident," I said.

"I am sorry to hear it." He led us into a parlor and indicated a ledger lying open on a desk. I leaned over to write our names. "Our families have been friends and neighbors and comrades in arms for a hundred years," he said. "In the first spring of the first cotton our families came here together."

"He has told me a lot about those times," I said, feeling quite at ease now and glancing at my mother to see if it was beginning to come through at last.

"His infirmity becomes quite personal," he said.

"As it well can under the circumstances," my mother said. "It is at once the pleasure and the pain of living in old established sections."

"Yes," the man said. "And your section?"

"Settled more than three hundred years," my mother said.

"Our families were in Charleston before they came here," the man said.

"And before that?" my mother said.

"Lincolnshire," the man said. I was still standing beside the desk in that museum-like room so full of bell glasses and glass cases that I scarcely dared move my hands.

"Then our ancestors very likely fought each other in England," my mother said. I flushed for I could think only of the other Civil War.

"After three hundred years," the man said, "having fought each other, particularly in another country from which we are now both exiled, makes for understanding." He took my mother's arm and conducted her out into the great hall. "Let us do the upper rooms while the light holds," he said.

We climbed the wide-sweeping stair into the upper dusk. The shaggy skin of a huge bear hung on the wall opposite the head of the stair. "Shot on this land," the man said, "while the house was building." When we had climbed up to the second floor, the skin looked less huge although it was still much larger than I. It smelled rather musty.

We passed the doors of several bedrooms. They were ordinary

rooms and clearly in constant use, for the beds were carelessly made, and small things lay scattered about—shoes, magazines, glasses with spoons, a shirt on a chair, a dress on a bed. The man called our attention to a picture hung between two windows. At first I could make out only a white blur, but as I stepped closer he said, "That white horse and the rider dressed in white took part in a famous race many years ago. This plantation was wagered against a street of houses in New Orleans. Our horse won, needless to say, and the house has never passed out of the hands of the family."

"It is like a story book," my mother said with just enough emphasis to let me know she was remembering *Gone with the Wind*.

"And this is the master bedroom." He opened the door gently and laid a finger across his lips before he motioned us to approach. Even then he allowed us only to cross the threshold and stand inside the tall room. The light there was very good, for one side of the room was almost entirely window, great twelve-foot windows that came right down to the floor. In the room was only a huge four-poster bed with its bare poles looking for all the world like a ship tied up at dock and stripped of all its gear. From the haphazard arrangement of the covers on the bed I could make out at least six patchwork quilts mounded up. At first I thought the bed was empty, but at last I saw the top of a head with a few strands of very long white hair. As we stood quietly, there was a faint stirring of the covers and a cough began, a small, hopeless, incredibly aged cough. My mother moved as if to step forward, but the man had already turned toward the door as if anticipating our leaving.

Once out in the corridor he stood beside the door for a moment as if listening to the muted cough. "The bed is the last of the really good pieces," he said. "We were all born in it and God willing we will all die in it. She is the last of those who really saw the great men here in this very house, the giants." The cough still went on as we passed down the corridor.

The man took down a bottle from a shelf as he went and shortly stopped beside a ladder going up to a trap door. "This looks like an ordinary decanter, doesn't it?" He held out an ordinary-looking decanter.

"Yes," I said.

"But note the rings around the neck," he said, running his finger over three pronounced ridges on the neck of the bottle.

"Ah," my mother said. She bent forward for a good look.

"It was the custom," he said, "to keep track of the number of drinks by pouring the first round from the one ring decanter, the second round from the two ring, the third round from the three ring."

"How interesting," my mother said.

"Furthermore it was held to be an advantage to have the rings for gripping as the hand grew more unsteady, if you pardon the allusion, ma'am."

"I hope I'm never so drunk I can't pour from any smooth-necked bottle," I said. I was getting impatient with this tourist stuff.

"Or keep your car on the road," my mother said.

"They were real men in those days," the man said. "They drank hard but it didn't hurt them because they worked hard too."

"I thought they were more of a leisure class," I said.

"In the same way that the men who run US Steel and General Motors are leisure class," my mother said.

"Exactly," the man said. "The responsibility was terrific and a most self-sacrificing effort had to be made to render a strict account of the stewardship."

"Naturally," my mother said.

"If you feel able to climb the ladder, you will be able to see the land they once worked," the man said. I wondered whether I should go up and leave my mother there or pretend to have no desire to see. It didn't at once occur to me that I wasn't being consulted.

"I haven't traveled a thousand miles to be stopped by a ladder," my mother said. The man sprang up the ladder and opened the trap. He climbed on up through the shaft of dust-filled light into the room above.

My mother spoke softly to me. "Is there a charge for going through the house?"

"Yes," I said.

"Have you given him money?" she said.

"No," I said.

"How will you do it?" she said.

"Wait," I said, although I was hard put to wait myself. That part of the protocol I knew letter-perfect. The man appeared again at the top of the ladder, reaching down to encourage my mother to climb. She climbed slowly and steadily. I followed close behind but she didn't need my help.

As I stuck my head up through the trap I felt the warm close air and smelled the dusty smell of summer attics at home. The cupola seemed not to have been invaded for a long time, so it had quite a different quality from the rest of the house.

The man turned slowly and looked out of one after another of the four windows. "All this," he said. "Where the town is. The lumber mill. The cotton gin. All those small farms. From the river—" he gestured toward a distant line of black trees—"to the mountain." Great blazes of light on the mountain seemed to indicate the windows of houses reflecting the setting sun. "And from a river you can't see to a road that no longer exists." As he spoke we all three of us turned slowly around like figures on a clock— not one of those clocks where the figures just move out and back but like the clock in Herald Square where two bronze men appear to beat alternate strokes on a bell to tell the hour. We moved like those men who appear to have independent action, but actually are governed by one mechanism, not like those others which are mounted on one platform and don't even appear to have independent action.

"Magnificent," my mother said. I wanted to ask him how

much land still went with the house and what had happened to the
rest, but I couldn't do it.

The sun went down into the earth like a hot penny into butter.
The man turned from the west window, and reversing our order
of precedence we went silently back down the ladder.

Out again on the wide porch in the surprising light of evening,
we stood quietly but not easily, for the time had come for me to
begin the gambit that would clearly establish my knowledge of the
inner working of things. To me knowledge of this gambit was
better than knowledge of the house and the land. It was better and
more valuable than all the courses at the University. It was even
better than having my mother there, but at the same time it was
worthless unless she was there to see it.

"A beautiful house," I said. I was lying. To me it was un-
painted, dirty, dark, and filled with ragged quilts.

"It has been called one of the finest of its sort," the man said.

"A very fine sort," my mother said. She had no way of knowing it, but what she said worked perfectly into the pattern.

"I had never before seen it at this hour," I said. That was Judge
Wilder's remark. At whatever time of day we came, he said the
same thing. We never went into the house but sat on the porch
or around back under some trees, and looking off over the rolling
land he always said it while he and the man nodded slowly together.
On my own I added, "It has a kind of special magic."

"It is always satisfying to show a treasure to those who appreciate it."

"Thank you," my mother said.

"It is hard to show proper appreciation for what you have given
us today," I said.

"Nothing," the man said. Until now he had been cautious, fear-
ful that my moves might be simply accidental, but now he relaxed
and followed easily, almost automatically, the steps of the formula.

"It is I who must regret not being able to show my appreciation of your understanding."

"Is not understanding given and received," my mother said, "the finest sort of appreciation?" I thought for a moment she had ruined everything. I was completely at a loss, but the man was equal to the situation.

He kissed my mother's hand.

I'm damned if I know how he got her hand or how she yielded it. I'm sure she never had her hand kissed before. I certainly admired him for that. On impulse, usually drunken, I have attempted to kiss the hand, but I have always fumbled and the hand has been stiff or else it has clutched mine so passionately that I could do nothing.

"That is indeed the soul of civilized behavior," he said, "but there are certain amenities involved in our traditional hospitality."

"We couldn't dream of inconveniencing you, sir," I cried.

"I insist," he said. "But what am I saying? I was just explaining to you that I could not extend the courtesy of the house."

"Have no regret," I murmured.

"Just before you came I discovered that we were out, absolutely out, of whiskey." The play was almost completed but I knew that I must not be too precipitate, so I remained silent for the proper moment of sadness. "I had just sent a boy—he was not yet out of sight when you drove up—down to the bottoms to our private still. It will be at least an hour before he can return. In the meantime you must be deprived of the rights of guests." He looked so incredibly mournful at this point that for a moment I found it hard to believe that he knew as well as I did what I was going to say.

"If you will permit it, sir," I said.

"What is this?" he said listlessly from the very depths of melancholy.

"I hardly dare presume," I said.

"In the face of my failure as a host," he said, "one may very well presume."

"I see I have offended you," I said.

"Forgive me," he said. "I meant no offense."

"Nor I," I cried. "What I was about to suggest," I said with an ingenuous rush of good feeling, "was that I happen to have some whiskey in the car—" I allowed my voice to trail off as if abashed at my own forwardness.

His face shadowed and lightened. "In the name of hospitality I accept," he said.

I ran to the car for the whiskey, and then he took it into the house while my mother and I sat on the sagging step. "Is this how you were going to handle it?" my mother said.

"This is how it is handled," I said.

"If you had given him the money, he would have been able to buy food," she said.

"Not by bread alone shall man live," I said. And I had her there. I had her there. It was as if I had finally said what I had been trying to say all day. I had found my shibboleth and I was at last released from my labor. It is nice to think I once thought the world so easy.

We stayed for the one drink that protocol demanded and then left him for his personal use what solace was left in the bottle although judging from the drink he passed me there must have been very little. As we were leaving he drew us around to the shaded side of the house and from the low branch of a great magnolia picked one last perfect blossom. He gave it to my mother, who cradled it in her cupped hands and inhaled the heavy scent as one might approach a rare brandy—and yet it was more like a priest sniffing the sacrificial wine.

"I had hoped—" my mother said. "But it seemed so late after I got here—and now—" She stopped trying and let it trail off into silence. I was too embarrassed to speak. The man said nothing but kissed her hand again with the same magnificent finesse and handed her into the car. We drove off without another word and without looking back. My mother sat stiffly with the flower resting in her hands resting in her lap.

My mother was quiet for a long time as we drove on in the darkness which was by now complete. In fact she only said one thing all the way back to the city. We were passing through a small town and I had to stop for a red light, so I took my eye off the road long enough for a good look at her. She was just sitting there staring ahead. The magnolia was still cradled in her lap, but I could see by the light of the street light that it was already blotched and brown. When she became aware that I was watching her, she made a visible effort. "The julep cups were sterling silver," she said. "Not by bread alone shall man live." I don't know whether she knew it or not, but I think she had me there.

The Appointed Hour

It was late at night. The summer was almost over. In a few days we would be back in our places all over the country, but still another night we sat up in The Barn hoping to hear something that might yet make a difference somehow.

The Barn had, of course, once been a barn. It even smelled faintly of hay. It was wide and tall, and at night it gave the feeling of sitting at the bottom of something, a canyon perhaps or a forest of huge trees—there were birds, swallows and some pigeons.

We were silently watching a fire go to pieces in the large stone fireplace. (The mountain nights were cold, so the fire was by no means sheer affectation.) A blackened log dropped from the andirons, broke open, and showered forth gold and sudden flame.

The poet Robert Hatcher roused himself and said, "First and last we've talked a lot about writers—that's what we're here for,

I guess—but they were all unusual in some way—unusual as successes or as failures. Tonight I'd like to tell you about a very usual sort of writer and about the very unusual circumstances that led up to my not meeting him." Hatcher drank from his bottle and passed it out into the dark for those who had no bottle of their own.

While the bottle was going around we settled ourselves to hear about this writer of Hatcher's. We would have preferred to hear about Hatcher himself, for, strangely, he was almost the only prominent contemporary poet who had not been analysed at length by at least one of our lecturers. It isn't that he was so outstanding a poet, but he was right in front of our eyes every day, and naturally we wanted to know about him.

As a matter of fact, although Hatcher was pretty usual as poets go, there was one way in which he was quite unusual: he seemed to feel he owed us something very special. After his lectures he would patiently answer questions as long as there was one person left to ask them. And at night he made it a point of honor to be among the last to bed. He would sit up drinking whiskey with anyone who wanted to talk with a successful poet, hear him and ask him questions. Perhaps Hatcher, who himself before his success had attended lectures and conferences and had invariably come away disappointed, wanted to try to give us something to take away with us.

"The name of this man I never met is Steven Pratt," Hatcher said. "By the way, none of you know where he is now, do you?" There was no answer. Hatcher struck a match and for a moment his face and hands hovered glowing over the pipe. He was blond and lean and just past looking young. Beyond that he looked like any man lighting a pipe, solemn, portentous, almost oracular. He waved the match out with a quick gesture of his wrist, and in the dark his wicker chair creaked as he settled himself.

"Before I really begin the story," he said, "there are a few things I want to tell you about Steven Pratt. I could easily hide these things from you without affecting the essential story—we've all written enough to know that—but, you see, I want to be honest with you. Or I could hide them only until after I had caught you with some gaudy beginning, like this, for instance: Steven Pratt went to bed drunk at three o'clock in the afternoon. When he woke up his watch was stopped at six o'clock. He didn't know if he had slept three hours or fifteen hours or twenty-seven hours, but he rushed out to try to keep his appointments because he knew that his job depended on his keeping appointments.

"Yes, I could have done that. I could have even made him a something in TV or an advertising man or an air force officer, perhaps, or some other kind of man people like to hear stories about, and that wouldn't have changed the meaning of what happened to him, but the truth of the matter is that Steven Pratt was an instructor in the English Department of Upstate University. Now I have told you that, perhaps you will go away. I really couldn't blame you if you did. The audience usually goes away when anyone tries to tell a story about college professors, English professors particularly. People—including me, and you know how long I taught English before I was able to make a living out of poetry or rather out of being a poet—people find it hard to believe that English professors have real lives, real wants and hopes and fears and loves, and not just ideas of lives and wants and hopes and fears and loves they got out of books.

"I could hide and change and contrive, but as I say I want above all else to be honest with you and win your confidence—how can I win your confidence except by being honest with you and telling you exactly what happened, as I understand it, even including the things which may send you away and leave me here talking to myself?"

As Hatcher paused to give emphasis to his rhetorical question, a man out in the dark said, "May I ask a question, Mr. Hatcher?"

"Certainly, by all means," Hatcher said. He seemed to be used to people who talked back to rhetorical questions.

Chairs creaked and there were quiet footsteps moving toward

the door, the soft heavy thud of a woman walking in her stocking feet and the barely audible whisper of crepe soles. The brief silhouettes at the moon-filled doorway clearly showed a man and a woman.

"Somebody must have taken you at your word," a different man said. A woman laughed nervously.

"There's a time and a place for everybody's everything," Hatcher said. "This time is for all of us, but this place is for me." He added quickly, "Don't be surprised if you see that in a poem some day—or is it from a poem I've written already?" The number of laughs was surprising. At night The Barn had a way of seeming empty. "But the question," Hatcher said, "what is the question?"

"Mr. Hatcher," the man with the question began, "what you say about being honest with us is all very flattering." Hatcher apparently recognized both the tone and the phrasing, for he began methodically to knock out his pipe, thwack, thwack, thwack, against the heel of his hand. "But I would like to know one thing: when you speak of honesty, are you referring to poetic honesty or practical honesty?"

"Both," the wise and seasoned Hatcher said, refusing to be drawn into a debate on the nature of truth.

"Very well," the man said, but still he pressed on. "Specifically I want to know if Steven Pratt is another name for Robert Hatcher?"

"A shrewd guess," Hatcher said. "Very shrewd. But it happens not to be right although I must confess that on this point—if it were true—I wouldn't hesitate to sacrifice what you call practical truth. You will soon see, however, good reason for believing that there are two of us, OK?"

"OK," the man said. It clearly wasn't OK with him, but at least he kept quiet.

Hatcher's pipe was drawing well now and he returned to his

story. "I mentioned that Steven Pratt was at Upstate University, didn't I? Upstate was really a small college with a lot of students. Each time I spoke there I got the feeling that every GI who ever wanted to go to college was on that campus. That isn't strictly true, of course, but there were thirteen or fourteen thousand of them at the peak. And for all those extra students extra faculty was needed. And that's where Steven Pratt came in.

"But Steven Pratt came in by accident, as it were. He never intended to be an English professor—perhaps that will make him more believable as a hero. He didn't know exactly what he wanted to do. He knew he didn't want to be a something in TV or an advertising man or an air force officer, but beyond that he just didn't know. He thought he would take some graduate courses while he was making up his mind. At that particular time, however, Upstate needed instructors more than graduate students, so Steven Pratt went to work as a full-time instructor and a part-time graduate student. On the side he wrote when he could and was rumored to be working on a novel. That, I think, is the last bit of information I have to force myself to tell you. From now on I can simply go ahead and tell you exactly what happened.

"Since writers are perhaps even more unbelievable than professors, I might have been tempted not to mention the writing except that this must have been the thing that first prompted him to write to me—that business of working on a novel off in the interior all by himself and the terrible sense we all have in the interior of having no one to talk with, no one who has the least conception of what we're trying to do or cares in the least about the things we care about. I had been there myself so I recognized the signs at once in his letter.

"It was easy to see that he was just about stir crazy. He had been sitting up there eating his fingernails and wondering if his novel was any damn good at all and if he was about to lose his mind. And then here was this poet coming to the campus. It must have maddened him to think of a poet being right there and un-

approachable—for he must have known my schedule—you know
what happens to poets on those campuses: lecture at 3:30, cocktails
at 5:00 (at Upstate it was with the modern literature and criticism
wing of the English Department), 6:30 dinner with the chairman
of the English Department, usually a philologist or medievalist or
Shakespearean—not that there is anything against those people, but
imagine how Steven Pratt would feel—8:00 informal discussion
with the faculty club, and then, if you aren't saved by a train schedule, 10:00, more cocktails with a select group of Mathematicians,
Philosophers, and Sociologists, associate professors probably, and the
people who think of themselves as the intellectual Young Turks of
the University.

"It must have been in sheer desperation that Steven Pratt wrote
me a letter, a simple humble letter saying in effect that if by any
chance I got to town early enough he would be delighted to have
me for lunch along with one or two others who were interested in
writing. (I discovered later that the 'one or two others' were actually
a couple who had an apartment more suitable for a small lunch than
Steven Pratt's one room.) But my god how do they make the time
for writing, these university people? I know I did it myself once,
but there doesn't seem to be any time any more.

"I wish I had been able to see his face when he got my note
accepting his invitation. I myself have written just such letters and
mailed them feeling, 'Well, now I have done everything. No one
can blame me for not trying.' I know I would have been amazed
to get a reply to such a letter. I really think I accepted his invitation as much as anything as a gesture toward those old letters of
mine. This was, after all, almost the first lecture I gave, and his
letter was the very first letter of that sort I had ever received.

"For some reason as time passed the lunch assumed great importance in my mind, and my trip to Upstate became a trip to meet
Steven Pratt, and my lecture became an open letter to a young man
who wants to write.

"When I arrived at the station I was taken in tow by the couple at whose apartment the lunch was to be held. The young man, it turned out, had once had a poem in *Duodecimo*. Steven Pratt sent his apologies and promised to join us immediately after his eleven o'clock class. He didn't dare dismiss his class so much as a minute before 11:50 because twice already that fall other members of the department had complained about the noise his students made in the corridor when he let them out early. They hadn't complained to him but to the chairman of the department so that each time it meant a formal reprimand and a formal black mark against him. There were other black marks as well: for not getting to class on time and for not keeping his office hours. And the students, like his colleagues, had gone straight to the main office. It was very kind of them to ask after his health, but there was always someone in the office to hear the question. And such things got around. With another drop in enrollment expected and another cut in staff as a result, such things were bound to get around.

"The apologies and explanations that I had on the way back from the station were only the first of a long series of apologies and explanations that kept coming in all day and all night to account for the continuing non-appearance of Steven Pratt. Between these explanations—virtually everyone I was introduced to had an explanation even after I learned better than to ask for one—and a long letter from Steven Pratt some time later, I know pretty well everything that happened to him both before he got drunk and after he woke up to make that ridiculous mistake.

"Imagine, if you can, a young instructor with an armful of books and papers walking as fast as possible across campus and even being grateful for stairs he could run up or down without attracting undue notice. Thanks to his letter I even know what Steven Pratt was thinking as he crossed the campus. He was thinking about another instructor at Upstate named Jay Burrage—his letter was most particular on that point. (Since I am committed to telling the entire truth, it would be well for me to admit that Jay

Burrage was a public figure, and like all public figures he was in
large part a product of public imagination—Steven Pratt's imagination included.) He was worried about Jay Burrage because he knew
that this little lunch was just the sort of thing Jay Burrage would
find out about and crash and turn into a virtuoso piece for his own
charm and eccentricity.

"It was possible, however, that Jay Burrage wouldn't be up yet.
It was as much as his reputation was worth to be seen in public at
that hour. He had all his classes scheduled in the afternoon and
even had his office hours in the evening in order to cherish his
precious reputation as a picturesque character. Even with his hours
arranged like that he still missed classes and didn't keep appointments. But nobody reported Jay Burrage. Jay Burrage was a lov-
able character, and everyone loved him and cherished his eccentricity
as much as Jay Burrage himself did.

"I haven't been able to discover any real evidence that Jay Burrage was any brighter than any other bright young man, but the
chairman of the department loved him. The chairman would even
loan him nine cents or thirteen cents or whatever other sum he was
cadging at the moment. I have heard that Jay Burrage would
even go around boasting that he never had to pay anyone back
because no one could remember loaning sums like that. In anyone
else it would have been a scandal, but people would fondly say, 'Oh,
Jay, he's a character. You should have seen him promoting twenty-
three cents from me the other day.' I can understand Jay Burrage,
believe me—we all know the kinds of things you have to do to
become a character—but I can also see how he would look to Steven
Pratt, who seems to be quiet, intense, drab, and entirely unlovable.

"At the door of his friend's apartment Steven Pratt forgot Jay
Burrage and thought only of meeting a poet. Can you remember
your first poet? Robert Frost was mine. He was just what everyone's first poet should be. It was just like going to church. I still
keep expecting poets to be like that when I meet them.

"When Steven Pratt could keep his mouth closed and breathe properly, he opened the door. I had indeed got there before him, but he didn't learn that at once.

"At first he was aware only of the massed backs of people, of loud and confused talk, and of almost impenetrable cigarette smoke. Then (he says) he saw my face through a momentary rift in the shoal of backs, but so fleetingly that he afterwards wasn't sure he had really seen it. As he stood futilely on tiptoe in the doorway, making little hops to see over the crowd, someone tapped him on the shoulder and said, 'Excuse me.' Steven Pratt mumbled an apology, and the newcomer, who was vaguely familiar, possibly a Philosopher or a Sociologist, moved briskly into the room.

"As if in a nightmare Steven Pratt groped along the wall of backs, looking for an opening into which he could insert himself, but he traversed the entire room and wound up standing in the kitchen doorway, making little hops to see over the crowd. Someone tapped him on the shoulder and said, 'Excuse me.' Steven Pratt moved aside mumbling apologies, but the person caught his arm. 'Am I glad to see you,' the person said.

" 'Oh, hello,' Steven Pratt said, only half taking his eyes off the backs of heads but recognizing the master of the apartment.

" 'Come out in the kitchen for a minute,' the master said. He clutched Steven Pratt's arm and drew him backward into the kitchen. 'Look,' he said, and pointed to a table littered with glasses, ginger ale bottles, and, most significant, two empty whiskey bottles. 'It's all gone,' the master said. 'Every drop. Who would ever have thought all these wonderful people would really come? And they're all here. All the people. In my house.'

" 'Mm, yes,' Steven Pratt said. It must have flashed across his mind then (I could have told him this myself) that in the future it would be just as well not to trust in the understanding of a person who has had a single poem in *Duodecimo*. 'But Hatcher, is he here?' Steven Pratt said, 'I thought I saw him.'

" 'Even Hatcher.' Steven Pratt turned to go back into the living room, but the master clutched him by the arm. 'We need more whiskey,' the master said. 'I've got to stay with my guests. Here's five dollars—every cent I've got in the world—and the car keys. You better get two bottles. We can straighten out our shares of the expenses afterwards.'

"Steven Pratt accepted the money and the keys and worked his way along the backs toward the door, moving always, but always trying to see through the crowd. Then a man with an empty glass in his hand turned and faced him—it was the junior member of the modern literature and criticism wing of the English Department. As the junior member stepped from ranks, Steven Pratt thought suddenly that his chance had come. He moved forward, but the junior member stopped him. 'Why, Steven,' the junior member said, 'glad you could make it. Having a good time?' Then, without waiting for a reply, the junior member went on to the kitchen while Steven Pratt was still nodding his head, unable to speak, unable even to arrange a smile on his face. He turned back to the hole left by the junior member, but the ranks had flowed together like smoke after it has been broken.

"Steven Pratt opened the door to go out but stepped behind it while the chairman of the department walked in (as if all doors always opened automatically for him) closely followed by Jay Burrage. 'Where is the master of this house?' the chairman boomed as he entered the room.

"'Out here,' the junior member called from the kitchen doorway.

"'Great idea, this informal lunch,' the chairman said without breaking his stride. 'Shows real spunk.' Steven Pratt was then able to come out from behind the door and go about his business."

"Mr. Hatcher," a woman said quite close at hand in the dark.

This was unexpected and a little weird. It was as if we suddenly heard directly the voice of a woman in that room Steven Pratt had just left.

"Mr. Hatcher," she said again in the small stir of restless movement that followed, "how did you feel about then? I think I can understand Steven Pratt."

"Good," Hatcher said. "Why, that's wonderful because I want you to understand Steven Pratt. It's very important that you understand him."

"Yes, Mr. Hatcher," a man said, "how did you feel?" The restlessness stopped, and it was clear from the silence now as well as from the questions that Hatcher was leaving out of his story the very thing that was of most interest to his audience.

"I felt mad," Hatcher said. "I thought I had been had. I didn't believe there really was any Steven Pratt. When all those people piled in there I was quite sure someone had pulled a dirty trick. I was getting quite drunk too because there was no lunch after all. Well, the chairman of the English Department finally got me out of there, and I was just drunk enough to ask him what the hell went with this Steven Pratt gag. The way he said, 'Oh, Pratt again,' soft and sad like a regretful judge passing sentence, made me wish I hadn't spoken, but then I could only tell him the whole story, and he kept saying, 'Oh,' like shooting arrows into a hanging man.

"Anyway, I was gone before Steven Pratt got back with the whiskey, but it was some time before he learned that. He only realized that the smoke was thicker than ever, that there were more people than ever, and that the solid phalanx of backs had broken down into small huddles with no space at all between them. But by squeezing and pushing—he had sampled the whiskey as soon as he was safely in the car outside the liquor store and again when he stopped the car at the apartment house and again freely at the door of the apartment—he was able to get into the kitchen and hide one bottle under the sink without being observed. It wasn't long, however, before people began wandering out with their empty glasses, and the two fresh quarts disappeared as only other people's whiskey can. By the way, any of you other people out there got any bourbon? I seem to be fresh out, and all this drinking Steven Pratt

is doing is getting me thirsty." A bottle was passed up to him and
he took a small drink to moisten his mouth and absently set the
bottle beside his chair.

"It was from Jay Burrage that Steven Pratt at last learned that
I had left the party. Sitting on the kitchen stool finishing one with
old Steven just to be sociable before he took a fresh one back to
the living room, Jay Burrage said, 'Too bad he had to go so soon.
Must be tired, though. Needs rest.'

" 'Who's this?' Steven Pratt said.

" 'Why, Hatcher,' Jay Burrage said.

" 'He's gone?' Steven Pratt shouted. He had been sampling
while he mixed.

" 'Yes, long ago. Damn fine of you to give up a chance to
see him, running errands, mixing drinks, and like that, though.'

" 'How come he went?' Steven Pratt said, sampling quickly.

" 'Our thoughtful chairman,' Jay Burrage raised his glass in
salute, 'thought he might like to lie down before his talk this afternoon. Damn thoughtful of him too. Hatcher looked bushed already.' Jay Burrage accepted a refill, the last of the bottle, and
went out to spread the sad word that the whiskey had run out.

"For a short time Steven Pratt did a small business in fresh
ice cubes and soda, all the while sampling the secret bottle under
the sink, but at last people bitterly acknowledged that there was
no more stretch left in their drinks, and they all went home. Of
course, the master of the house was still there and his wife and
Jay Burrage, who was going around looking into empty glasses,
draining drops, sucking cubes—it was all part of his being a character.

"The master and the mistress opened all the windows and
all the doors and went out to eat while the apartment aired. Steven
Pratt sat on the kitchen stool contemplating chaos. It was there
that Jay Burrage found him when he came out to inspect the glasses
in the kitchen and the empty whiskey bottles. 'Aha,' Jay Burrage

said, 'Steven Pratt on the throne. It's no good lying, Steven, where did you hide it?'

"'Hide what?'"

"'The bottle, man. No good mixer ever leaves himself mixless. That's why I came looking for you.'

"Without a word Steven Pratt produced the bottle and handed it to Jay Burrage, who took it, felt it, held it up to the light, sighed, and said, 'I knew I could count on you, Jay boy. You have a nose for such things.' That too was part of his being a character.

"It would also have been like Jay Burrage to sit drinking other people's whiskey rather than go to the lecture. Only the whiskey didn't last that long, and when it was nearly gone Steven Pratt gathered up the other empty bottles and took them out in the hall to the incinerator. One by one he dropped them, listening with sad pleasure as they bumped down the sides until they broke, some sooner, some later. Then he dropped down ginger ale bottles and Coke bottles. Then all the milk bottles there were in the hall. He had his hands full of glasses when the master and mistress came back. 'Couldn't do a thing with him,' Jay Burrage said. 'A wild man.' As a matter of fact Steven Pratt had been remarkably quiet and preoccupied all the while, and Jay Burrage—why, he didn't say a word or make a move but just sat on the stool watching from the moment Steven Pratt first began to collect the bottles. Well, Jay Burrage squeezed the bottle one last time. 'Got to get along to the lecture,' he said. 'Want some help with him?'

"They must have wanted some help with him because they were all in Steven Pratt's room putting him to bed at three o'clock in the afternoon. Although he was weak his head was clear. He was even aware that Jay Burrage was managing to convey the impression that this was an old story to him (poor Steven, you know) but he was too busy to bother about that. Flat on his back on his bed with only his coat and shoes off and his tie loosened, he said, 'But I can't go to bed. I have to go to the lecture. And I have to go to the cocktail party to explain everything to him.' He struggled weakly to get up, but Jay Burrage held him down while the others quietly left the room.

" 'Take it easy,' Jay Burrage said. 'Rest a little.'

" 'No, no,' Steven Pratt said. 'I have to see him.'

" 'You'd better not.'

" 'Why not?' Steven Pratt said. He tried again to get up, but now he could only twitch his arms and legs aimlessly. 'Why not? He said he'd like to see me. I have a letter.' He groped at his breast for my letter, which, he says, he always kept in the inside pocket of his coat.

" 'Rest a little while anyway,' Jay Burrage said.

"Steven Pratt was by now unable even to speak, but he could clearly see Jay Burrage leave the room, and he could hear laughter in the hall."

Hatcher again moistened his mouth with whiskey and sent the bottle around as if it were his own. "Mr. Hatcher," a man said, the same man as before, "may I ask a question?"

"Certainly," Hatcher said. He apparently recognized the voice, for he began the slow steady thwack-thwacking of his pipe against the heel of his hand.

"If you are being truthful—and it is, of course, we know, the responsibility of the *vates* to be truthful—how then is it that you can reproduce conversations that you never could have heard?"

"You forget Steven Pratt's letter," Hatcher said, "and my remarkable memory."

"I only mentioned it," the man said, "because of your initial emphasis on truthfulness."

"I made up a lot of it—the dialogue, that is—but it's true just the same."

"Ah, poetic truth," the man said. It was easy to imagine him nodding his head as he spoke and long afterwards.

"I can show you the letter if you like," Hatcher said. "I have it in my room."

Far away a rooster crowed, and in the barn over our heads a sleepy bird twittered. The bottle came back to Hatcher and he took another drink. "There is a gap in the story now," Hatcher said, "at least as far as Steven Pratt is concerned. Things went about as planned for me. I tried very hard—perhaps too hard—with my lecture because I wanted my stock to be high if I should get a chance to put in a good word for Steven Pratt. I felt in a way responsible for what had happened and would happen although Steven Pratt himself writes, not once but three times, that he considers me to be completely without blame. (He speaks of my non-involvement, the same quality he found in my poetry.) But as it happened I never did get a chance to speak up for him because no one would bring up the subject. They were all as tactful as could be once they were sure the damage had been done.

"Now back to Steven Pratt," Hatcher said briskly as if hurrying his thoughts back from far away. "He is waking up in his room. Suddenly and completely he is awake. His hand automatically lashes out at the alarm clock, and then he lies there waiting for the soft click of the shut-off mechanism. Every morning he is awake just before the alarm is supposed to go off, and every morning he presses the button and lies waiting for the click, at which time he will spring into action. He is so conditioned to the sound that sometimes in the evening while he is reading or correcting papers the clock will click and he will find himself half way to the door with his books in his hand before he realizes what he is doing." Hatcher hesitated. "You see," he said, "he told me everything in those long unanswerable letters. In an effort to make me understand, he told me all the things I could never have understood unless I had understood from the beginning without any explanation at all."

"Mr. Hatcher," a woman right at his feet said, "are you shifting to the present tense in order to indicate a shift in pace in your story? I am interested from a point of view of technique."

"I didn't realize I had," Hatcher said. "I didn't mean to."

"I thought you might be trying for more immediacy," the woman said. She hesitated over the word *immediacy* as if it were new to her, perhaps picked up in one of the day's lectures.

"I didn't mean to at all," Hatcher said. "I'll try to be more careful."

"I'm very sorry, Mr. Hatcher," the woman said. "Please do go on."

"Ah, yes," Hatcher said, "of course. There was no sound from the clock, so Steven Pratt picked it up and looked at it. It had stopped. He sprang out of bed and ran to the bathroom to soak his head. Exercising an iron self-control, he even shaved his still numb face without great harm to himself.

"As he came out of his house, his practiced eye noted that the light had that peculiar gray that it has when the sun is still just under the horizon. Judging from the light he thought he probably was on time, but just the same he decided not to take the time for coffee, much as he needed it. It was, however, with very real regret that he passed the Varsity Coffee Shop because one of his few pleasures was to be the first each day to sit at a certain table, a table neat and spotless until he sat there and drank coffee while students, assistant professors, associate professors, full professors, department heads, administrative officers, janitors, football players, coeds still slept. Even the bright young men, who the chairman of the department thought were brighter than Steven Pratt, still slept. This knowledge was perhaps the only compensation for being assigned the office hours 7-9 A.M.—that and a clear track to the bathroom while he was getting ready.

"But he did pass the Coffee Shop and went on about his business, and this very shortly brought him face to face with the Temporary Office Building, a loutish building set squarely in the middle of the campus on the fine grassy quadrangle around which the permanent buildings had been built. Like the other temporary buildings, this had formerly been part of a monstrous army camp.

The buildings had been dismantled at the camp and set up on the campus. You could look at some of the other buildings and recognize them as barracks. People who knew about such things called one a theatre and one a chapel, but the squat squareness of this particular building gave no clue as to its former use. It had been set down exactly at the point of intersection of all the worn paths cutting across the old quadrangle, and many students, particularly on rainy days, following their ancient paths like lemmings, walked in one door and out the other through the one huge room that took up the whole interior.

"This building was the first thing put up in all the post-war expansion at Upstate. Even before a single GI showed up, the paper work was enormous, and this one huge room was filled with rows and rows of desks for the clerical staff. Well, the clerical staff finally moved into the Permanent Office Building, but the Temporary Office Building stayed in use because despite all the paper work and all the planning no one ever visualized anything like the demand for office space. In fact things got so bad after a while that the desks in the Temporary Office Building had to be used in relays because there was no ground left on the campus and no time in the master schedule for the construction of new office space. Oh, that was a big operation and a tight schedule. But even so, at any given moment there would be hundreds of men striding with determined strides back and forth from one building to another, in and out of laboratories and libraries, up and down stairways, not because they had a great deal to do, but rather because they had nothing to do, and they had to look busy. They had nothing to do because they had no desks to work at. This was understood by everyone at the school, even the biggest wheels in the administration, and the only thing a man had to do was look busy until it came his turn to use one of the desks. That was how things were done at Upstate.

"For a moment Steven Pratt was filled with panic at the thought of being late again. He still had no idea what time it was, but he was a little reassured by the fact that day had even then not yet broken. It occurred to him, however, that the sky might be overcast, threatening rain. That would account for the increasing gloom, and he might be very late indeed. But he was fully reassured when he entered the Temporary Office Building and saw, even from the door, that there was no cluster of students milling around his desk. He stood in the doorway catching his breath.

"He says he always used to consider that there were ten rows of ten desks each in that room, but when he came to make me a diagram so I could see exactly how it was, he discovered this wasn't true at all, and he remarked that every morning all year as he came through that door he was confronted by a large 28 painted on the first desk in the middle row and that his own desk was 41, the fifth desk in the first row to the right of the middle row.

"The lights in the room seemed even more night-like than the exterior darkness, and he thought again of the approaching storm. He regretted not having brought his raincoat, and as soon as he stepped out of the open air he regretted having got up at all.

"All over the room desk lamps spilled puddles of light across the floor. Steven Pratt had to walk through a number of these puddles to reach his desk, and each time the light touched his feet, the man at the desk looked up grimly, the light falling harshly on his face. None of the men were familiar to Steven Pratt although he felt that by that time he had a nodding acquaintance with most of the men who used at that hour the desks he had to pass to get to his own.

"Fortunately there was no student seated beside his desk when he got there, so he was able to sit down for a moment to get his bearings. He looked back toward the door and counted the desks he had passed. There were nine. None of the nine men, neither those whose faces had stared out of the light nor those who had looked coldly over the shoulders of students seated beside the desks, had seemed familiar, but with the headache he had that wasn't too surprising. No one had smiled or nodded. No one had said good morning. There had been nothing other than the same look of blank hostility he himself gave strange students as they walked toward his desk—and then past on their way to the library.

"The way he felt it was no more than he would expect that people would scowl at him, but still he was worried because those men were all the kind that would smile no matter how he felt. On ordinary mornings they all smiled or nodded. There were even two who said, Good morning, Pratt. And that one assistant dean said, Good morning, Steven, just because they happened to share a table at the cafeteria a couple of times.

"He was only too well aware that his getting drunk was just the sort of thing to be spread around in some fantastic version or other, and he wondered what all these people had heard about him that led them to reject him so completely. The fact that he was altogether disgusted with his behavior didn't make him any readier to accept their attitude—they probably came to the wrong conclusions from the wrong evidence anyway. But even then did they have the right to reject in him—even if they did know everything—what he was obliged to reject in himself? What is tolerance but the forgiving in others of what in oneself is unforgivable?"

"Mr. Hatcher, please, sir," the woman at his feet said, "who said that last, you or Steven Pratt?"

"Why—" Hatcher said. "Well—" he said. "It is hard to tell, isn't it? I guess I said it when you come right down to it," he said. "I hope you people don't belong to the school that won't let a poor author have a word for himself in his own story."

"Oh, no, Mr. Hatcher," the woman said. "I just wanted to know."

"I'll try not to mix in the story any more than absolutely necessary," Hatcher said. "Steven Pratt still was hoping for some sign of recognition, and he spun his chair slowly, his eyes travelling successively over the desks immediately around his. Slowly his eyes swept over 31 and 32, whom he had passed and who still didn't look familiar, the one now seen half from the rear, left, and the other in profile, left. Then he looked carefully at 33, 42, 51, 49, 40: half profile, left; full face; half profile, right; profile, right; half rear, right; rear, respectively.

"And although each raised his head as the chair turned toward him, attracted by the motion or the gentle creaking, none of them looked familiar and none of them smiled. They all stared directly ahead, observing with what marginal vision they could and listening for what they couldn't see. Only 42, directly behind him, looked him full in the face, but even 42 seemed too absorbed in contemplation to acknowledge his presence as much as did 40, the back of whose head expressed an amazing degree of attentiveness.

"Steven Pratt let his feet down and stopped himself when he had completed his swing. He drew his chair up to the desk. With a scowl he read a note saying that one John Croft might be late for his appointment. He crumpled the note fiercely and flung it at the wastebasket. He could remember no Croft in any of his classes, but doubtless he would know the man if he saw him. He took a set of themes from the top left-hand drawer—his drawer. For just a second he was afraid it might not be his drawer. Everything had been so strange that he might well be in the wrong building at the wrong desk. Of course he knew that there was no other building even remotely like this, but still he checked the typewritten schedule which was scotch-taped squarely in the middle of the top of the desk. The English Department was assigned this desk at this hour, seven to nine—he glanced at his watch, which was, of course, still stopped—and the top left-hand drawer was its drawer. Middle left, Citizenship, 9-11. Bottom left, Math, 11-1. Top right, Romance Languages, 1-3. Middle right, Philosophy, 3-5. Bottom right, Psychology, 5-7. The middle drawer belonged to Chemistry, 7-9 in the evening.

"Although he was at first relieved and reassured by the schedule, Steven Pratt soon realized that the schedule only stated that this desk belonged to the English Department at this hour and in no way stated or implied that it belonged to him. However the themes that he held in his hand turned out to bear his section number and his name: Mr. Pratt, Dr. Pratt, Professor Pratt, Herr Doctor Professor Pratt. Some of that foolishness was done on purpose to irritate him because, of course, they all knew that he was neither doctor nor professor. The two themes at the bottom of the pile even had comments he remembered writing the day before while he was waiting for a student. He read through the comments with an unpleasant awareness of how they might look to the chairman of the department if a student were to go to him and say, I don't have to stand for anyone writing things like this on my paper. Carefully he tore off those parts of the pages on which he had written, reminding himself of his standard remark to a class at the beginning of the term: If you get back a paper with part of it torn off, that means I wrote something on it that I decided I didn't want you to see. Sometimes he would save himself the trouble of putting his opinion into words and would tear off large pieces of the paper without writing any comment.

"Reassured that even if all wasn't well he was at least in his place, he spread the papers over the desk and set to work.

"Do you hear that? He set to work. Everything was wrong—the time, the place, the way he felt—but he set to work just the same. He snatches a minute and sets to work.

"He found it necessary, however, to switch on the lamp before he could really see the papers. He thought briefly of the approaching storm and looked apprehensively toward the window, but sitting there in his puddle of light he could tell nothing about the state of the sky.

"He tried to read a paper explaining the non-appearance of angels in modern times, but he was reading so slowly that he couldn't remember what he had already read. The words passed through his mind one after another, orderly but meaningless. He was so absorbed in contemplating himself trying to read this freshman theme that he didn't notice the coed settling herself in the chair beside his desk until she was actually seated and meticulously smoothing her skirt over her careful, knee-clenched lap. 'Ah, yes,' he said, detaching himself with great difficulty from the paper, 'your folder, Miss—' He left his sentence hanging in the air and held out his hand.

" 'Folder?' the girl said as if he hadn't said every day to every class that students must bring every word they had written every time they came for conference.

" 'Folder, Miss—'

" 'Emrich,' the girl said. 'Emma Emrich.' Although he never could remember their names, he would have sworn that he never could have forgotten this one.

" 'Well, Miss Emrich,' he said, 'there is no point in talking further.' He sighed and passed his hand over his forehead, feeling obliged to say just a bit more, to temper his severity if only with further severity. 'You know the rule. How many times do you suppose I have told the class the rule? And I have always been careful to explain that as much as I would like to do more I have only time, because of our crowded facilities, to speak to you concerning your papers.'

" 'But I never—' the girl said.

"He made a slow gesture of tolerance although his hand was becoming unbearably heavy. He smiled sadly. 'My dear young lady, if I were to allow myself for one moment to listen to your tale of woe, inside of one week I would be swamped by everyone on this campus who has a tale of woe to tell, not only my own students but everyone else's. I would be completely kept from doing my own work, the work I am paid to do and the work I am qualified to do: help with your composition.'

"The girl tried again to speak.

" 'No, no,' he said, standing up. 'You must go at once. There is someone else waiting.' The girl began to cry, her mouth opening and closing soundlessly. 'No,' he shouted and pounded his fist on the desk, 'no tears. That won't work. Get out of here and wash your face.' He swayed on his feet and saved himself by sitting down suddenly. The girl was on her way to the door before he had finished speaking."

Outside The Barn but very close at hand, a woman laughed loud and clear. Hatcher stopped and listened. "Come in," he called. "Come in." There was no answer but the screen door squeaked slightly and that was all. Hatcher drank from the bottle he had kept beside his chair and passed it out into the darkness to find the newcomers—if any.

"This new difficulty, with students now, drove Steven Pratt into a frenzy. 'Sit down,' he shouted at the boy who was standing beside the chair the girl had just left.

"The boy sat down, twisting his body in order to look after the girl, who was just going out the door. He turned back leering.

"Steven Pratt made a great effort at self-control and said sharply, 'Sir, it would be more becoming if you were to pretend that you knew nothing of that unfortunate girl.' The boy gaped. Steven Pratt gestured raggedly at the huge room and said, 'These intolerable conditions make it impossible to preserve the traditional secrecy of the conference desk. Under these conditions one must act with circumspection and not allow himself to see or hear that which it is dishonorable for him to know. Your folder, sir.'

"Scarcely disturbing the O of his mouth, the boy said, 'Huh?'

" 'Folder. You know the rule.'

"The boy seemed to shake himself and grow in size and hardness. 'Where is Mr. Croft?' he said briskly.

"The very irrelevancy of the question checked Steven Pratt's first impulse to violent speech and gave him time to remember the note that had been on his desk when he came in. 'There was a note saying he would be late.' Then suddenly resenting having been tricked into a soft tone and an irrelevant subject, he said, 'And I would appreciate your not using my desk as a clearing house for your inane messages.'

" 'Mr. Croft—'

" 'Croft me no crofts,' he shouted, 'and fold me your folder.'

" 'I have no folder,' the boy said.

" 'Then what are you wasting my time for?' He felt an almost uncontrollable impulse to rest his head on the desk and go to sleep, but with a great effort he forced himself to go on. 'You know the rule.' Each word he spoke was almost too much, for to speak at all he had to move a great weight that rested on his chest. After each breath he felt he would not again be able to move the weight. 'There can be no exceptions.'

"The boy was sitting back and watching him craftily. Steven Pratt became more alert for a moment, but the heaviness of his head and hands and the weight on his chest kept dragging him down toward the desk. A thought which was intended to be secret was routed down the wrong track, and he found himself saying, 'Don't think you can trick me with silence and cunning into saying and doing what I don't want to say and do.'

" 'Of course, sir,' the boy said, managing paradoxically as he said it to seem more silent and more cunning than ever.

"Once he got his elbows on the desk, his head in his hands, Steven Pratt felt absolutely immobile, solid as the oak veneer office furniture. 'You may go,' he said without looking up. One of his elbows slipped a trifle with a loud squeak. He could tell that the boy wasn't leaving. He rolled his eyes so he could look at the boy without disturbing his head, but he could see only as high as the boy's shoulder.

" 'You will leave,' he said, wrestling mightily with the weight on his chest and feeling that this was his last strength and that if the boy chose to ignore his command there was nothing he could do about it. He closed his eyes to rest them and left his command hanging in the dark, the command invoking all the force of the university, uttered as it was by the appointed man in his appointed place at his appointed hour. In the darkness of his closed eyes he was comfortably aware of the firmness of his desk and the firmness of his own strongly braced position.

"There he was," Hatcher said, "sitting in the dark, hanging on and hoping. Do I need to say what he was hoping for?" There was silence as if Hatcher were really waiting for an answer. "I'm glad I don't because I don't know. Steven Pratt himself probably didn't know either. Some sort of miracle I suppose. And do I need to add that he kept his eyes closed in order to put off as long as possible seeing what you always see when you open your eyes after sitting in the dark, hanging on and hoping for a miracle?" Again there was silence.

"Steven Pratt opened his eyes. The boy hadn't left. More than that, standing in line behind the boy were another boy and girl. Steven Pratt turned his head enough to be able to see the face of the girl. With a start he sat up. 'Get out,' he shouted. 'Must we go through all that again? Don't come back until you can bring your folder and then only at the proper time: when you have an appointment.' The girl didn't cry and she didn't leave. The boy sat cunningly in the chair.

"'What's going on here?' the man standing said—Steven Pratt, when he looked at him, could see he was more of a man than a boy.

"'Well may you ask,' Steven Pratt said. 'Well, indeed. My students have all gone mad. That's what's going on here.'

"'What's the big idea?' the man said, getting red in the face and stepping closer. 'What's the big idea, anyway?'

"'Idea, indeed,' Steven Pratt said. 'Mad, that's what they are.'

"'What's the big idea sitting at my desk, bullyragging my students, making girls cry? There, there, Miss Emrich,' he said hastily to the girl, who was standing there hard-eyed. He patted her on the shoulder, and she smiled quickly although they both continued to stare at Steven Pratt.

"'Your desk, your students,' Steven Pratt shouted automatically." Hatcher paused a moment, just long enough to pick up the bottle and take a drink.

"Steven Pratt heard a small chorus of squeaks and looking up saw all the swivel chairs at all the desks turning toward him, all facing him full face, not only the first circle of 40, 31, 32, 33, 42, 51, 50, 49, but out beyond that all the other numbers in concentric circles clear to all the walls of the room.

" 'My desk, my students,' the man shouted. He shoved his red face down close to Steven Pratt's.

" 'Every day all year seven to nine desk forty-one,' Steven Pratt shouted, pounding the schedule on the desk with his fist.

"The man started back and then smiled, oh, so cunning. Appealing to the room at large, he said, 'Every day this year I have sat at this desk at this time and have conferenced my students.' Steven Pratt, despite his excitement, winced at the synthetic verb.

" 'He sat down as if he owned the desk,' someone said.

" 'He spun around in the chair,' someone else said. Steven Pratt turned quickly, trying to locate the speakers, but they spoke too briefly for him to find them.

" 'He shouted at her.'

" 'He threatened her.'

" 'He made her cry.'

"Despairing of meeting these accusers, Steven Pratt tried to concentrate on the red-faced man, who seemed to be less angry now than amused and confident. 'We can't both have sat here at the same time every day,' Steven Pratt said, trying to be reasonable.

" 'No,' the man said, 'so why don't you leave?'

" 'This is the Temporary Office Building, is it not?'

" 'Yes,' the man said.

" 'This is desk forty-one, is it not?'

" 'Yes.'

" 'It is between seven and nine o'clock?' Steven Pratt suddenly realized that he didn't have any idea what time it actually was, and he felt a quick stab of fear.

"But the man said, 'The time is exactly 7:45.'

"'Then I am right and you are wrong. Just look at the schedule.'

"'Now you look here,' the man said, beginning to lose his temper again in the face of this ruthless logic. 'I have looked at the schedule every day this year, and this desk belongs to me at this hour.'

"'There is no need to lose your temper just because I prove you wrong,' Steven Pratt said, very calm and remote.

"'Get out of here,' the man shouted.

"'Now, now.' Steven Pratt was tired but he smiled tolerantly. 'Suppose we ask the gentlemen at the other desks. They cannot deny, despite their unkindness to me today, that I have always sat at this desk at this hour.'

"'Ask them,' the man shouted. 'Go ahead.'

"'He smelled of liquor when he came in,' someone said.

"'He has been falling onto the desk,' someone else said.

"Steven Pratt was furious. He shouted, 'Never mind irrelevant slander. Who belongs at this desk at this hour? That's all I want you to say.'

"'John Croft,' someone said.

"'Good old John,' someone else said.

"'Every day.'

"'Seven to nine.'

"'Always a kind word.'

"'Hello, John.'

"Steven Pratt spun his chair toward the sound of each voice, but he was unable to see anyone actually speaking.

"'Now will you leave?' the man said triumphantly.

"'It's a trick,' Steven Pratt said. 'I will not leave. I am right.'

"'Very well, you asked for it.' The man laid his hand on Steven Pratt's shoulder, 'Come on, boys,' he said. They all stood up and moved in. Circle on circle of them, closing in around the hard-eyed girl and the silent boy to get at Steven Pratt. He clutched the arms of his chair and waited."

Hatcher waited too. In the lengthening silence, the woman at his feet began, "Mr. Hatcher—"

But Hatcher began again abruptly, perhaps just as she spoke or perhaps just a trifle after, and drowned her voice as if she had been playing Wedding Guest to his Ancient Mariner. "My god," he said, "can't you feel things close in? Don't you cross your fingers and pray for Steven Pratt, hoping for prayers when your time comes?"

He waited again. "It's darker than ever in here," he said.

"The fire has gone out," the woman at his feet said.

"The moon has gone down," a man farther out in the dark said.

There was another brief silence and Hatcher's voice came suddenly, very loud. " 'Just a minute,' someone shouts. 'Hold on a minute.' Everything stops except for a mole-like ripple in the ranks that works its way to the center and finally reveals Jay Burrage. 'What's going on here?' Jay Burrage says.

" 'Who the hell are you?' says the man who claims that Steven Pratt's desk belongs to him.

" 'I'm in this man's department. I know him. He isn't well.'

" 'He made my students cry,' the man shouts, waving his arms and advancing on Jay Burrage.

" 'I use desk sixteen at this hour,' Jay Burrage says very calmly. 'Harry, Whitey, Craig, and Morphitt and the rest over there will vouch for me.'

" 'Is that right?' the man shouts as if he will personally have Jay Burrage lynched if it's a lie. Far on the other side of the room several men stand up on desks for a good look.

" 'That's old Jay,' someone calls.

" 'Prince of good fellows,' someone else calls.

" 'Always a good word.'

" 'Any friend of Jay's.'

" 'OK,' the man says, his whole attitude changing. 'OK, Jay, you see how it is. He must be having some kind of hallucination.'

" 'I know,' Jay Burrage says. He shakes his head sadly. 'Very sad. A most promising bright young man. These aren't his hours at all, as I happen to know. You can see for yourself by the schedule that he has no business here now.'

" 'Good,' the man says. 'Can you get him out, Jay?'

" 'I'm sure I can, John,' Jay Burrage says.

"Steven Pratt tries to speak, but the words get lost inside him, and he sits quietly in the chair. 'Come on, now,' Jay Burrage says, turning to Steven Pratt. 'You'll be better off in bed than down here trying to do your job while you're not well.'

"It infuriates Steven Pratt that Jay Burrage should try to humor him, but he can't think what to say. He gives the chair a short quick turn to the left and then to the right and then faces Jay Burrage, tense and silent.

" 'Tell you what, Steven. I'll stay here and take care of your students if you like,' Jay Burrage says.

"Steven Pratt slumps in his chair. He sees, in a sudden flash of insight, Jay Burrage sitting down at his desk and talking with his students and then all his students letting the word get around how much better they like Jay Burrage and how much more he knows. He wants to protest but he knows he is too sick. 'It doesn't matter,' he says. 'They're all mad anyway.' Jay Burrage helps him to his feet. 'This doesn't mean,' Steven Pratt says in a final effort to save his pride at least, 'that I concede your right to this desk at this hour.'

" 'Quite right,' the man says. 'We can straighten this out when you feel better, Steven, old man.'

"Leaning heavily on Jay Burrage, Steven Pratt starts toward the door. 'Just a little more,' Jay Burrage says. 'Lean as much as you want.' Steven Pratt begins to get the feeling that he is walking down into the floor and that the floor is rising around him like water. 'Buck up, man,' Jay Burrage says. 'You're lucky I found you

before there was real trouble.' Steven Pratt is well aware that all
this talk is just to keep him going, like talking to a beat horse, but
he is too tired even to resent it. 'I didn't plan to come by the office
at all tonight,' Jay Burrage says, 'but I stopped off for my pipe on
the way to the club for Hatcher's talk.'

" 'Is he still in town?' Steven Pratt says, reviving suddenly.

" 'You knew he was speaking tonight.'

" 'Last night he spoke.'

" 'No, no, tonight,' Jay Burrage says. 'You're all mixed up,
Steven. It was only about five hours ago that we put you to bed.'

"Steven Pratt believes him at once. Everything is now clear—
at least many things are. 'I can still see him then,' Steven Pratt says.
He becomes so excited that he almost walks by himself.

" 'You'd better not.'

" 'Why not?' Steven Pratt says, steadying himself in the doorway. 'He wants to see me. I have a letter.'

" 'I know all about that,' Jay Burrage says, 'but still you'd better
not go.'

" 'He wants to see me,' Steven Pratt says. He stumbles off the
top step.

" 'Now look,' Jay Burrage says. 'Ever since noon Hatcher has
been asking for you.' "

"A lie, a god damn lie," Hatcher shouted. "I didn't. I wouldn't."
His voice began to trail off. "Wasn't I trying to help him?"

The Barn was dead quiet and very cold. I was shivering as
violently as if I had heard a ghost shriek. Hatcher's bottle banged
loudly on the floor as he set it down.

Hatcher continued the story at once, as if he had never spoken
out, as if, in fact, he believed he had only thought it was a lie. " 'Do
you hear me, Steven?' Jay Burrage says. 'Our chairman is blowing
his top about your inviting Hatcher and then not showing up yourself. I'll tell him that you're sick—that you've got a dose of this
twenty-four hour stuff that's going around. I'm not a very good

liar, but it's the best we can do. If he saw you now or heard what happened tonight, you'd really be through. So go home, Steven. Get some sleep. Lie low.' Jay Burrage steadies Steven Pratt on his feet and starts him off across the campus."

There was a flutter in the air around Hatcher's head as a bird, which had forgotten the way out of the barn, flew distractedly in circles. Hatcher waited until he was sure that the bird wasn't coming back again, and as he waited I became aware for the first time of figures in chairs and on the floor. It was still too dark, however, to be quite certain if any of them were awake.

"Well," Hatcher said—he sounded suddenly very tired—"Steven Pratt went out onto the campus. The campus was very dark, which surprised him at first because he was still hoping, despite his knowledge, that the sun would be rising soon. He steered first for the mass of the chapel which lay across his way. Reaching the chapel, he leaned for a moment among the dry leaves of the ivy on the wall. For the time being he was much too tired to continue home, so he moved along the wall to a dark angle and lay down under a bush to rest a while.

"He lay on his back and forced his eyes to stay open while the earth revolved majestically under him and tipped further and further until there was very real danger of his falling off.

"Out of all the varied images of the day there appeared to him, vividly, the picture of himself standing back to hold the door while the chairman and Jay Burrage swept into the room. He remembered exactly how accomplished a liar Jay Burrage was, and he knew intuitively exactly what kind of a lie he would tell the chairman.

"There was a blinding glare of light that for a moment frightened Steven Pratt. Gradually he remembered that it wasn't morning but night and that at night huge flood lights illuminate all dark corners of the campus until the coeds are shut up safe in their dormitories. Even when he closed his eyes he couldn't escape the great illumination, so, groaning heavily, he got to his feet and went home.

"I might add that Steven Pratt was exactly right about the kind of lie Jay Burrage told about him, but that was little consolation. Neither was there consolation for Jay Burrage because he lost his job in the spring too: someone must have been telling lies about him.

"I would like to think it was Steven Pratt who told those lies about Jay Burrage, but I don't believe it. He doesn't strike one as being a liar—there are some who aren't—a few—but as for the rest of us, give us this day our daily lie, for the one we tell today will make it easier to tell the one asked of us tomorrow."

There was a silence that lengthened until I was certain that everyone, including Hatcher, was asleep, but still I felt that something ought to be said, some few words spoken over the open grave of Steven Pratt. "There never was any further word about Steven Pratt?" I said. That wasn't at all what I wanted to say, but at least it wasn't nothing.

"Nothing," Hatcher said. He didn't move in his chair and he seemed slumped in sleep. "He had no one to say goodbye to, so no one knows where he went, but he was seen at the station carrying a suitcase and a book and the box that was rumored to contain his novel." Hatcher sat up abruptly. The wicker of his chair shrieked. "My god," he said, "do you suppose he did manage to salvage something and that after all that he is somewhere by himself off in the interior working on his novel? I tell you I look in the book review sections on Sunday with a mixture of hope and fear—if he does do it—well, I don't know, that's all. I just don't know. I don't think he will but he might. He just might. I don't like to think about it.

"I have a lecture in the morning," Hatcher said. "I'll have to rest a little." He stood up and walked directly to the door. No one in The Barn moved or spoke.

Hatcher stumbled across the daylight at the door, but he gave no sign of seeing it. Neither did he lift his head toward the morning streaming up from behind the hills. Still dazed by the night in The Barn, he walked as straight as he could home to bed.

William Sanders and the Dream of the Future

Of course it's hard to remember now, but there was a time when television was new in the land. People read about it and talked about it and waited for it to come to them. It was to be a marvel.

No one read and talked and listened to travelers' tales more avidly than William Sanders. No one in secret dreamed more golden dreams. But he wasn't one to go out. He would wait. Nothing could be clearer—or so it seemed to him and to all who knew him.

The first thought, however, that crossed his mind when he was ordered to drive to the Boston office to go over the books was that he would see television. This seemed to be nothing short of divine providence, this gratuitous opportunity to be a seer of marvels and a teller of tales.

Divine providence—or something else—had already, years before this, provided William Sanders with a wife: it seemed like a good idea at the time, he would tell himself whenever he happened to catch himself wondering. So although his dream of television was intensely private, he knew that the dream bed had to be shared. He could even have predicted her first words about his trip if it had occured to him to doubt them enough to speculate.

"Well," she said, "when do we have to leave? What do we have to take? It's a pretty time of year for a drive, and if we're careful we can make your expense check cover both of us."

He handed her the memo that told everything. "Yes, it will be a pretty drive," he said, "and there probably isn't anything really wrong with the Boston books, not with poor Gilbey's books."

"Perhaps we'll be able to make a swing around by Providence and visit Aunt Sally," she said.

He made a noise that might have been yes or no or perhaps, but neither of them was listening.

When they began to get into the country around Schenectady, he slowed down so that he could look around more carefully. From what he had read, a bar would be the likely place, so he scanned each bar carefully for the unmistakable signs, which he could not fail to recognize from pictures and advertisements. And when he saw his first television antenna, he did recognize it at once, and he very nearly stopped there, but the place was much too clearly just a bar.

He did stop shortly at a bar and grill. "I need some coffee," he said to his wife. "Would you like some?"

"Go right ahead," she said. "I brought some mending." She took from her knitting bag a pair of his ragged shorts, a blue striped pair he had never liked even if they were a wonderful bargain. As he was getting out of the car she was experimentally laying out on the shorts a scrap of an old green house dress. Who's to see it? she always said. And of course she was right.

With his first step inside the door he was glad his wife hadn't come in. She would never forgive him such a place. And with his first step he spotted the television screen. One step and one quick stranger's glance at the whole room and he knew where he would have to sit. Carefully he walked to the end of the bar and settled himself so that as he sat normally and relaxed, looking straight ahead at nothing in particular, the screen was full in his view.

A large man in shirtsleeves came out of the back somewhere and walked toward him. "Morning," the man said.

"Good morning," William Sanders said.

"What'll you have?" the man said.

Up until that very moment William Sanders had thought he could say coffee, but in the face of these domes of beer and lines of stiffly erect bottles behind the bar, he couldn't bring himself to say coffee. It was too sickeningly early in the morning for beer. "Whiskey," he said.

"Chaser?"

"Water."

Skillfully the man poured a heaping glass and, leaving the bottle on the bar near at hand, went about his business, checking his stock, bringing in and opening fresh bottles, arranging buckets of ice, bottles of juices and syrups.

William Sanders watched the bartender for a moment and then allowed his eyes to drift toward the screen. The dirty white screen was filled with dim and unidentifiable motion. It seemed to be out of focus. Resting his head on his hand so that he could hide his eyes, he stared hard to see what he had never before seen and had scarcely hoped ever to see.

But even by staring until his eyes ached, he could discover only that the motion within the screen wasn't quite so aimless as he had thought. The speed seemed to vary and the mass, but most of the motion was directly across the screen. He had to close his eyes without learning anything further, and with his eyes still closed he tossed off his whiskey.

When he again opened his eyes, the bartender was working close under the screen with his back turned. William Sanders cleared his throat loudly. A face, quite clear, sprang into the screen. The face moved and spoke. "What'll you have?" it said.

"Whiskey," he said, startled.

The face disappeared from the screen, and an aimless motion began as the bartender came along the bar and poured the whiskey.

Having grasped the fact that the set was turned off and acting as a mirror, William Sanders amused himself for a while identifying the reflections in the screen as trucks and cars passing on the highway and the bartender working around the bar. He even took a trip to the men's room so that he would be able to find himself in the dirty screen when he was moving. Then he drank his whiskey and went on his way.

"Well," his wife said, stuffing his shorts into her bag, "you were long enough about it. Another five minutes and I would have finished the whole thing."

"Yes," he said, "it took a while."

"You've been drinking," she said.

"There wasn't any coffee."

"You didn't have to stay."

"It's not that easy," he said.

"For you nothing is ever easy," she said bitterly, "but I'll make this as easy for you as I can: so you just stop at the next diner we come to and get yourself some good strong black coffee. This is one trip you aren't going to get drunk on and spoil everything."

Saving him from drink was one of her favorite gambits. Actually in the twenty years they had been married he had never been drunk, had very rarely had so much as two whiskeys. But way back, before they were married even, she had formed the idea of him as one who needed to be saved, and even twenty years' experience had done nothing to banish the illusion—not that he hadn't had provocation, god knows.

She was clearly working up to a major effort, so he huddled up inside himself in case there was anything left to protect and struck himself deaf with an old husband's trick. Of course he could still hear her. No trick is perfect, but just the same it helped, like a device to take off some of the electrical current and keep a machine from burning itself up.

She said: "If I hadn't kept right after you ever since I met you, you'd be just like the rest of the men in your family—a little Irishness they call it but I've seen them carried home from wakes and weddings and baseball games and fishing trips—and pay days, my god, every pay day, your father and your brothers and that lecherous old uncle of yours and those other uncles too and don't think I haven't seen the bruises on the women, from falling against a stove they say or tripping over a rug as if their floors were ever that polished or on the ice, a likely story indeed, and now you're drinking again. Well, I sha'n't stand for it. No more of that. Your grandfather's wake indeed and your mouth full of whiskey instead of prayers for the old sinner (God rest his soul) who was just like the rest of you to the end." She stopped.

Although naturally he didn't mention the fact, it was quite clear to him that he really needed coffee, so he picked a diner where a dozen big trucks were pulled up. "Good," his wife said, "I read in one of my magazines—oh, I meant to cut the article out and bring it on the trip because it was full of hints about trips—and it said that where the big trucks stop you will find good food and strong coffee. Bring me out a cup, will you?"

"How will you have it?" he said. Although she always had it the same way, it would never do for him to assume she wanted two creams and two sugars because that might cause her to remember he had forgotten she was supposed to be watching her weight.

"The usual," she said.

"Two and two," he said. "Don't you want to come in?"

"No," she said. "I don't like those places, and besides I want to finish those drawers I started to patch."

He immediately regretted picking this diner. He felt as if he had stumbled into a club in which the members were too polite to ask him to leave. He drank his coffee hurriedly. It was really strong but not very good. He noted with experienced eye that the television set wasn't turned on. As he was paying, he felt obliged to say something, as if he thought everything was quite all right, so he asked about the road to Boston.

"Twenty still closed?" the cashier called to the drivers huddled around a pinball machine. She was really a very pretty cashier, and if he had been a truck driver he would have drunk that lousy coffee every trip too.

"Still closed," a man said although none of them looked up.

"Better take Five," the cashier said. "There's construction on Twenty."

"Gee, thanks," William Sanders said. "I sure wouldn't want to get mixed up in that." The marked map his wife had got from the touring service had showed a long stretch of construction on Route Twenty near Pittsfield. "Thanks a lot, fellows." No one answered but he felt he had made an adequate exit.

He pushed on then through the Albany-Schenectady area without stopping again. They ate lunch in Massachusetts at a Howard Johnson's where a fake television set made of cardboard announced the special of the day to be fried Ipswich clams. They weren't bad either. In the afternoon they stopped for gas at an isolated garage where there was only an old hand-operated pump. While they were waiting he fished two bottles of orangeade out of the icy water of a cooler. And then they came to Boston.

They went directly to their hotel, both of them tired from the trip and feeling unclean. But by the time he had showered and shaved he felt much refreshed. He stood by the window seeing what he could of Boston. "I wonder what I'll find in Gilbey's books," he said. "Poor devil hadn't been a well man for years. Maybe that got to be too much for him. It doesn't have to be the books. In fact I'll be surprised—very much surprised—"

"Of course," she said, "and when that's over, we'll go around by Aunt Sally's. It would be a shame to be so near and not go."

"If there's time," he said. "I don't know about taking the time. Poor Gilbey."

"William," his wife said, "do you mind? I'm very tired. I think I'll lie down before supper."

But he wasn't tired or at least he didn't feel like making use of the other bed. "I think I'll take a walk," he said. "I want to look around a little, maybe find the Boston Common."

"Good," she said. She was already prostrate with a cold cloth across her eyes. "Find out where it is because I want to see it too. Perhaps tomorrow night after you get through work, I'll meet you and we'll go if I'm not too tired. I expect to be worn out from shopping. I can't wait to get at that fabulous bargain basement Pauline is always talking about."

All the bars displayed banners announcing baseball on TV, but by then it was too late for the game. He went into a bar anyway and drank a beer. "How was the game?" he said to the bartender.

"Those god damn Yankees," the bartender said.

"Was it really clear?"

"They got everything and then they got luck on top of that."

"How did DiMaggio look?"

"Just the way he looks every day. He's so good it hurts, the bastard."

William Sanders went from bar to bar hopefully, drinking a beer in each and then moving on. It isn't surprising then that before long he was drunk. And being drunk he found courage to ask directly about the idle set. "Isn't there anything on?" he said.

"Not much around this time of day," the bartender said.

"Could you give it a try?" William Sanders said.

"Something special you want to see?"

"No, nothing special."

"Not worth it," the bartender said.

William Sanders took himself off to the men's room. When he came back, the bartender was just stepping down off a chair set under the television shelf.

"There wasn't nothing," the bartender said.

William Sanders looked up quickly at the screen. A disk of light in the center was rapidly contracting like an iris, and then it blinked out. "It lights up bright?" he said.

"Sure it lights up bright, Mac. What do you think?"

"I don't know what to think," William Sanders said.

"Hang around, Mac, and you'll see something later if you just want to see something."

But William Sanders, very drunk then, had so far established the pattern of one beer to a bar that he automatically got up and walked out although he was in the very act of promising to stay.

He found himself much later seated at a crowded bar face to face with what seemed to be a television screen, but he couldn't tell for sure. There were no knobs or dials anywhere in sight. It was really like a window into another room or—because there seemed to be no focus or pattern of activity—perhaps it was a set not turned on, mirroring the bar in which he sat. He studied the bar and checked it against the screen. Definitely not the same. Of that he was sure.

What he could see was an empty stage in a night club of some sort. But there were all kinds of difficulties in seeing. The bartenders dashing back and forth kept getting in the way because the set wasn't placed up high like most but was down on the counter where the bottles were kept. And in the night club itself there was also interference. It must have had something to do with where the television camera was set up because every once in a while a waiter with a tray of drinks would completely block the view. Or the cigarette girl would walk right up to the camera, perhaps to talk to the cameraman, and her delicious bosom would fill the screen.

Bottles and glasses were constantly being set down and snatched away right where he was trying to look. Undoubtedly some kind of commercial—he had heard about these commercials. Very tricky indeed. It looked sometimes—but of course he wasn't used to television and above all he wasn't used to drinking—it actually looked as if the bartender (the very bartender who brought him his beer) was mixing drinks right there in front of him and then putting them into the television set. He couldn't believe his eyes. And then an arm came down and took them out the back. Of course they had the best brains in the country working on these gimmicks just so you wouldn't be able to believe your eyes.

About then the stage show got under way and he forgot to worry about the tricks. In spite of everything it was a fine view across the little stage. All the performers were seen from the side but very clear and very lifelike, far beyond his wildest imaginings of what television could do, better in some cases than actually being there, better at least in the case of the fan dancer who, holding her fans between herself and the audience in the night club, left herself uncovered to the camera.

Well, he was glad he was seeing television, but now it looked unlikely that they'd ever have it in their house—at least not until it was cleaned up a little, not that the girl wasn't manifestly an artiste, but, well, not everyone was so liberal as he.

When the master of ceremonies—your jovial emcee, he called himself—said the show was over and when the screen showed only a little dance band with couples dancing and lots of waiters blocking the view, William Sanders said to the man next to him, "Save my place," and hurried off to the men's room. All that beer, my word.

The next thing he knew he was in a night club of some sort. He had no sensation of losing track of time, but there he was hurrying out of the men's room—back to his place at the bar, he thought, but actually into the rear areas of a night club. He studied the place carefully. There was a little dance band on a little stage. Couples were dancing and waiters were racing around with trays of drinks. Yes, there was the jovial emcee seated at a table amid a throng of three couples of bobby soxers—well, the next older group anyway. Shows who's getting old.

He turned to look for the television camera, which he dearly wanted to see, and then he saw her.

She was seated alone at a table in the back. She still wore her feather headdress but was wrapped up in a long cloak from beneath which peeped only the toe of her delicious silver sandal.

He had somehow crossed the floor to her. She looked up at him sternly. He wasn't quite taken aback. "I want you to know," he said, almost overcome with beer and with emotion, "a wonderful future in television. You were magnificent." A hard word but he got it out perfectly.

"You really think so?" she said, smiling suddenly a smile that dropped more fans than he ever dreamed of. "Won't you sit down?"

He sat down. "Yes, sir," said the waiter at his elbow.

"A beer," he said.

"And the lady?" the waiter said.

"I'll have coffee, Carl," she said. "Two creams and two sugars." William Sanders started. She laughed then. "I have to watch my figure," she said. "It would never do to get scrawny, and dancing really takes the weight off you if you aren't careful."

"You can't be too careful," he said.

"Not in this business you can't."

The word business was like a signal that released suddenly for him an automatic pattern of talk and saved a conversation that was already beginning to lag. "How much longer does your contract have to run?" he said. "Is it renewable, and, if not, what are your other commitments?"

"Still thinking of TV?" she said.

"I rarely think of anything else," he said absently. Having begun to talk business, he now began to make a few notes on the back of an envelope.

"Now look," she said, leaning forward and clutching her cloak across her bosom, "are you really interested in TV?"

"Of course, I'm interested," he said. "It's the dream of the future."

"I tell you what," she said, putting her hand on his firmly (the cloak fell open), "if you're really interested—" She smiled shyly and clasped the cloak with her other hand. "If you're really interested" (he nodded violently), "come to my dressing room after the next show—that's the last—and we can go up to my place and talk contracts."

"Delicious," he said. "Delightful to find you willing to talk business."

She gave his hand another squeeze while she stood up, her cloak swirling about her, oh, god, endless legs, then settling as sad as marble. "I'll see you after the show," she said.

What a wonderful girl she was. Who'd think it? It was easy to see how a man old enough to be foolish, unhappily married—why, perhaps that was even what was wrong with the Boston books, if there was really anything wrong with them: a man in a position of trust, a girl like that only not really like that but looking like that only not wonderful—

Becoming very confused, he went to the men's room and mysteriously wound up back at the very bar where he had first seen her on television.

Ha, he must have been dreaming. That's it. A thing like that couldn't really happen to someone like him. Wait, he could recognize the waiter Carl ever so clearly on the screen. No, Carl must have been part of the dream, seen first on television and then dreamed into the dream.

Wait. There were the notes he took on the envelope. They might tell something. But the notes were just squiggles as if he had been pretending to write shorthand. Still he had taken notes somewhere about something even if they didn't make sense any more.

The problem was too difficult for him to solve, so he put his head down on his arm and watched the show go on. She was dancing now, much more aware of the camera than before, smiling at it, blowing it a kiss even, as if for him alone sitting there in front of one set out of a million sets tuned in.

Now, then, who was this large and spreading female walking across the dance floor, pausing in the middle to look around, turning toward the camera as if unaware it was there but like as not pretending and all the time wanting her picture to be flashed into a million sets—my god, it looked like—for a minute there—but of course that was impossible. But now she turns again and stalks toward the camera, bent as if to stare down its throat, and yes, my god, yes, larger and larger until her face fills the screen, his wife.

Then her face moves and she speaks, as if directly to him out of the million sets tuned in. "William?" she says tentatively. "William!" She keeps coming until her head and shoulders spring through the screen, and he faints.

"No, lady, no," the bartender said. "You can't crawl through the pass-through. Go around back by the rest rooms" (he drew a big circling diagram in the air), "and you're welcome to him if you want him."

He came to his senses immediately. He hadn't even fallen off the stool, but he pretended to be still unconscious. "William," she was whispering in his ear. "William, wake up. We've got to get home now. Tomorrow will be a hard day. William, are you all right?" He tried a little groan just to see what would happen. Her groan was louder and more heartfelt. "That's right," she said, "wake up now, and let's get along home to bed."

He sat up then and stared at her and nodded. She quickly slid an arm around his chest to help him up. He leaned more and more heavily until she let go with a sob. "Oh, William," she said, "please try to help yourself."

"Let me help you, lady," the jovial emcee said—everyone was standing around staring. "I'll help you get him into a cab."

"Look who's in a big hurry to get rid of him," the waiter Carl said.

"Look who's in a big hurry to shoot off his big mouth now," the jovial emcee said.

"Even with a mouth as big as yours you still haven't got what it takes to thaw out that ice-cold bonfire whatever it is he's got you haven't got it."

This was all lost on William Sanders. He hadn't seen the sign out front advertising his dancer as The Flame Dancer, and he hadn't noticed that her fans were flame-colored. But none of this was lost on his wife. She had seen both the signs and the fans, and her magazines had long since told her everything else she needed to know.

"Can it, the both of you," the bartender said, "and help the lady if you're going to. Don't louse him up any worse than he is."

"OK, maestro," the emcee said, "ring for a cab and give us a little run-off music."

"There's a cab outside," the bartender said.

"OK," Carl the waiter said, "let's hustle this customer's order, the both of us. Come on, Mac," he said, taking one of William Sanders' arms.

"His name is William," his wife said weakly, protesting automatically but without conviction.

"William," his wife said when they were alone in the cab. "William," she said weakly and possibly even timidly, "William, are you all right?"

He was braced for an attack. In anticipation he was leaning into it as one leans into a strong wind, and when it didn't come he collapsed all at once. "I'm tired," he said. "I'm terribly tired."

He was actually on the point of falling asleep, so she went on, trying to keep him awake. "I had an awful job finding you, but I knew you must be somewhere looking at television."

Wide awake he said, "Don't ever mention television again. I don't want ever to hear of it again."

"But, William," she said, "you're always talking about it yourself."

"I shall never mention it again." And he never did. "And I shall thank you never to mention it again." And she never did. "This will contribute much to our future happiness." And it really did. But he brooded sometimes.

The Score Keeps Changing

Everyone said there was a war on, and everyone who didn't get caught in the draft was making pots of money and having a good time—everyone, that is, except Ken Dean. Ken couldn't seem to find the right combination. He had thought, when he was teaching high school in Alabama, that all he had to do was drift down to New Orleans at the end of the school year. He had thought that an able-bodied man could always get a job, as a laborer at least, but just the same he didn't tell the school board he wasn't coming back because you can never tell for sure how things will turn out.

But once in New Orleans he discovered it wasn't that simple. He didn't have a trade that would bring him in a pot of money, and he had too much education to be hired as a common laborer at pay that might not be a potful but anyway was twice what he could make teaching school.

When he found out what the score was around New Orleans, he tried lying about his education and got a job as a bellhop, but he lost the job when the hotel found out through the F.B.I. that he had lied. The F.B.I. was checking on everybody in those days. And that was a job he could have had even if he told the truth, but they caught him lying. What the hell, he said. He would live off what he had in the bank as long as that lasted.

It was lasting pretty well, too, because he was moderate in his ways. He lived in a one-room apartment on the patio of an old French Quarter house. He did a lot of cooking for himself, and when he ate out he ate at a restaurant much frequented by artists, so this served in part as entertainment as well. He slept more than he had ever slept in his life, and he discovered the great joy of doing nothing.

Sometimes he would sit on the front steps of the house and watch people in the street. Sometimes he would sit on the door sill of his apartment and not see much of anything. Perhaps a woman washing her hair on a balcony or hanging out clothes. Perhaps an artist cleaning brushes or banging away at a piece of stone. Perhaps he would just see the great leaves of the banana trees and the dry fountain in the patio.

At night he would sit and listen to the sound of distant voices without words or the music of a string quartet crossing over the walls from the patio restaurant or laughter somewhere or the immemorial creaking of ancient bed springs. But whatever it was it was better than correcting papers or waiting on table or clerking in a store or reading his eyes out. The only catch was that his money would run out sometime, but for now he was happy in his discovery that a man doesn't have to work.

One day he sat in the doorway of his apartment doing nothing. He wasn't even smoking because he had run out of cigarettes and didn't care if he had any more or not—at least until he happened to be passing a store. He was just sitting there with his eyes half closed against the sun and half open so he could watch a girl hang out a wash in the patio. She had an apartment in the house proper, not in the patio wing, and she had come out of the house and passed him without seeing him. He watched her because she was something to watch, like a banana leaf in the wind or a bird scratching in the dusty fountain.

He had watched her before though God knows she was nothing spectacular. On the other hand there was nothing wrong with her. She was of average height and weight. Regular features. Dark hair and eyes. Her legs were good enough. The calf muscles knotted now at the edge of her dirndl skirt as she stood on tiptoe, and her average breasts lifted in her skivvy shirt as she raised her arms to hang the clothes.

Her name was Alice Walker. He had sat on the front steps and watched her come in and take mail from the box, and then he checked to see whose mail was gone. He learned a lot from post-marks and return addresses and sometimes by feel and by holding letters up to the light. From return addresses he learned that she heard from no men and that her family was in Little Rock. From a letter held up to the light he learned that Father was well. From a post card he learned that George had broken his leg and had been shot. From a letter providentially unsealed he learned that Father was in the lumber business, that Betty was working for her trous-seau and things while Tom was in service, and that they all still thought it was strange Alice was working in the shipyard and not coming home to be Father's secretary as they had always planned when they sent her to secretarial school. Alice had spoken briefly to Ken in passing, so he knew that her voice was soft and gentle.

"Oh, hello," she said as she turned from the clothesline. "I didn't see you sitting there."

"Hello," he said.

"You gave me a start," she said. Setting down the wash basin in which she had been carrying the clothes and clothespins, she reached up to her elbow among the folds of her skirt and brought out cigarettes and matches. "Cigarette?" she said.

"Thanks," he said. "I'm out."

She shook out a cigarette for him and then one for herself. She gave him the matches and he lighted them both. "Thanks," she said. "Got a job yet?"

"No," he said. "It's harder than you'd think."

"Oh, I know it's hard," she said. She sat down on the bottom step of the stairs going up into the house proper. "Don't be dis-couraged."

"I'm not discouraged, more resigned." He shifted a little so the sun would be out of his eyes and so he could see her better.

"That's bad," she said. "I haven't seen any of those cards from the U.S. Employment Service for you lately. Have you given up trying to get a job through them?"

"I guess they've given me up," he said.

She ground out her cigarette on the flagstone and flipped it toward the fountain. She picked up her basin and stood up. "How are you fixed?" she said suddenly. "Money, I mean."

"Well—" he said.

"I tell you what," she said. "Let me take you to lunch. I think I've got an angle for you."

"Oh, no," he said quickly. He wasn't ready to go yet. He hadn't by any means exhausted the possibilities of the patio for the day, and he hadn't sat on the front steps at all. Later, after he had sat on the front steps for a while, there would be time enough for lunch. The streets would be deserted then. Everyone would have gone inside to lie down. Then he could look through the mail at his leisure: read the post cards and the magazines, pull out the flaps on ads and circulars, try to see how much people owed and how much they were getting from home or allotments. Then he could eat. If Mr. Kaplan's *Life* was there, he could take it with him to read while he ate because Mr. Kaplan never got home until after 4:30.

After that a walk along Royal Street would be good, looking in shop windows. And wherever he was when it began to rain, there he would stay. He would watch people run close to the buildings, girls' faces washed by the rain. He would talk with those who could wait. He would go into the shop to look at pictures and books, to handle pewter and brass. There was a great deal to do. In fact there was so much to do that he would have no time for lunch with this girl who was trying to become more than something to watch.

"No false pride now," she said, and he knew he had protested too quickly. "I'm working and I can afford it, and besides my angle is so good you'll be working soon and can pay me back if it will make you feel better."

"Well—" he said. What the hell, he could watch her eat as well as anything, and he could listen to her talk although he preferred conversations in which a couple of other people had to think up the answers. And he would get a free meal he hadn't expected and an angle he might be able to use sometime when he needed it.

"Good," she said. "Wait right here while I run up for my purse."

"I'll meet you out front," he said.

"Good," she said. She ran up the steps and he could hear her sandals banging on the stairs all the way to the top of the house. Then he went around and sat on the front steps.

The mailman was not yet in sight, but he watched a cat on a fence and a beer truck at the corner bar. He watched a woman carry home the groceries and a man in pajamas standing at a window watching her. He watched two women talking on their front steps. He watched the old horse of a peddler stale at the curb. He watched a band of mourners bringing home the coffin from the funeral parlor to variations on the Perdido Street Blues played by trombone, clarinet, and sax. He watched from time to time the smoke rising from the pipe of an old man in shirt sleeves rocking away in a floor-length window across the street and watching him.

"I hope I wasn't too long," Alice said beside him.

"Not at all," he said. "I was just thinking."

"Shall we go?" she said. She had changed her skivvy shirt for a peasant blouse that was better for her shoulders and neck but not so good for her breasts. She had taken off her bandanna and combed out her hair, which was short, dark, and pleasantly disorderly. "Do you know M. Serramon?" she said.

"No," he said. "Is he your angle?"

"No," she said, "he has a restaurant. We'll eat there if you don't mind."

"Good," he said. "Sounds wonderful. I never even heard of him." It would be a change and wouldn't cost him anything. It was better too than if she had offered to take him to Antoine's, which he had heard so much about that it was bound to be a disappointment. Antoine's would be full of people who had heard about it just as he had heard about it and who would be so busy looking out of the corners of their eyes that they wouldn't be worth watching long. "Where is this M. Serramon?" he said.

"Over near the Cabildo," she said.

They walked east on Orleans Street and then through Pirates' Alley alongside the cathedral. Turning south past the Cabildo, Alice crossed the street obliquely and stopped before a curtained door in a nearly anonymous building. "Is this the place?" Ken said.

"Chez M. Serramon," Alice said. She waited beside the door.

The door was set flush in the wall, and the curtains made it look more like a window. There was no sign of any kind and the only mark anywhere on the building was a patch of faded red and white diagonal stripes painted on the wall beside the door. "I was always going to go in and ask for a haircut just to see what was in there. Now I'll find out." He opened the door.

They seated themselves at a table near the door. The cloth was covered brown with flakes of bread crust. There was a newspaper abandoned on the chair beside Ken, and he looked at it wry-necked while a large gray-haired man got up from another table where he had been reading, smoking, and drinking coffee. "Bonjour, monsieur," Alice said.

"Bonjour, mademoiselle," the man said. He sat down at the table with them.

"It is a nice day, isn't it?" Alice said. Still pretending to read the paper, Ken noted the change from Little Rock High School French to English.

"A very nice day," the man said. "What is your pleasure on this very nice day?"

"What but the dinner?" Alice said. "When I saw what a nice day it was, I said to myself, Who but M. Serramon will know what is good to eat on a day like this?"

"And if it had been a rainy day?" he said.

"I would have said the same thing," Alice said.

"Good," he said, "good." He took the cloth with him to the kitchen, and there was a great flapping of cloth and banging of pots and shrieking of French. But he was back almost at once with the clean cloth and great sticks of bread. Alice and Ken both broke bread, showering the cloth with brown flakes. Then the man was back again with the soup. He stood smiling while they tasted it.

"Good," Alice said. "Very good."

The man glanced at Ken. "Very good," Ken said. The man smiled and went back to the kitchen into the din of pots and of French.

Yes, the soup was very good indeed, a thick Creole gumbo. And the fish was good, a flaky white fish with a trace of sherry that came and went. And the light, golden omelet was good too, but Ken was beginning to tire by then and picked at it genteelly.

"Something wrong with the omelet?" the man said. He snatched a fork from the table and took a piece of Ken's omelet. He closed his eyes and tasted carefully. His soul was smeared all over his face. The omelet was clearly just what it was supposed to be although Ken himself had never tasted anything quite like it. "Ah," the man said, "eat it up. It's good for you."

"It's really delicious," Ken said, and he went doggedly on to finish it, but he groaned inwardly when the meat came on.

He was prepared to give his all on the meat course, but with the first taste his appetite returned, and he mopped up the last of the pepper and mushroom sauce with pieces of bread. He was even a little disappointed to see the peaches and French coffee placed on the table.

Ken gave Alice one of her cigarettes and took one himself. "Remind me to get some," he said.

"Keep the pack," she said. He put them in his shirt pocket. "Now for the angle," she said.

"I suppose there always has to be an angle," he said. He saw her start to frown. "Of course it's for my own good."

She smiled. "The man for you to see is Father Van."

"A priest?"

"Do you know where the priests live in the alley side of the cathedral?"

"Pirates' Alley?"

"No, the other one."

"Yes, I know now, but why a priest?"

"They're strong here. If you want anything done you go to the priests. After you've been here a while you come to realize that this town not only doesn't look like an American town but it isn't an American town in lots of ways, and this is one of them."

"What do you know?" he said. "I never thought of that."

"You couldn't think of that. We just aren't built able to think of that. Are you a Catholic?"

"Technically, I suppose."

"What does that mean?"

"I was born, baptized, communionated, and confirmed into the church, and they claim that means forever, but I haven't been working at it for years."

"You know the ropes though. You know to call him father and all that?"

"Oh, sure," Ken said. "That's built in, I guess."

"Good," Alice said. "Good. You'll be all right when you see him."

"Sure," Ken said. A lot of water might flow over the dam before he ever got around to needing to see Fr. Van. "I sure do thank you for the angle."

"That's all right," Alice said. "But we have to hurry if we don't want to kick it away."

"Hurry for what?" Ken said.

"I hope you won't mind," Alice said, "but I know how desperate you are for a job, so while I was upstairs I phoned and made an appointment for you. I guess my U.S.O. work gets me into the habit of just taking over everybody's business like that."

"The appointment is now?"

"Yes, but it's very near here. That's why I wanted to eat here."

"Oh," Ken said. She was being so damn cold-blooded about everything that perhaps after all she was just trying to be helpful. And despite the fact that he had been wary when he thought she had something else in mind, now he was piqued.

"That among other reasons, of course."

"Of course," Ken said. They went out again into the street, past the Cabildo and past the front of the cathedral, and into the alley where the priests live.

Alice bummed another of her cigarettes from Ken and waited for him to light it after he got through knocking on the door. He lighted her cigarette, and she said goodbye when they heard some-one coming to the door. Ken said goodbye too and turning himself saw her skirt swing as she turned and her calf muscles tighten and her heel lift off her sandal. Then he was facing the door, which was opening slowly.

It was an old woman who answered the door. "Good after-noon," she said. She was really very old, perhaps out on loan from the old people's home to do this pious work before the end.

"I have an appointment with Father Van," Ken said.

She led him to a sitting room and told him to wait. He could see her pulling herself up the stairs inch by inch, halting on each step to rest momentarily. Through the doorway he could see a steady stream of priests and people coming and going, but he couldn't even begin to conjecture about them. There were young people with books and briefcases, priests with books and briefcases, old women with armfuls of flowers, priests reading small books and feeling their way along, a young couple holding hands, a huge young priest striding, his robes lashing at his legs, whistling, two priests talking—French, he supposed.

"Ah, Mr. Dean," said the young whistling priest, who had popped suddenly into the doorway, filling it entirely except for a little space around his ears.

"Father Van?" Ken said.

"Yes," the priest said. "Sit down." He threw himself at a small chair placed sideways at a plain table in the middle of the room. The chair creaked loudly. The priest plunged his arm up to the elbow into the folds of his robe and came up with a sack of tobacco and cigarette paper. "Roll one?" he said.

"No, thank you, father," Ken said. "Have one of mine."

"No, thanks," the priest said. He began to shake the tobacco into a paper. "So you can't line up a job, eh?"

"No, father."

"What's your trade?" The priest snapped at the string of the sack with his great teeth, and with his free hand he pulled the sack shut.

"I'm a teacher," Ken said.

"Looking just for a summer job?" the priest said through clenched teeth, the sack swinging under his chin as he spoke and his hands forming the cigarette.

"That depends," Ken said.

"Mmm," the priest said. He took the sack from his mouth, licked the cigarette, sealed it, and put it in his mouth. "Depends on what?" He scratched a match on the under edge of the table, and it popped into flame as it appeared over the edge.

"Lots of things. Money isn't everything."

"It helps, though," the priest said.

"A lot," Ken said. "But I got the feeling I wasn't doing enough for the war effort. If I can get a job that will let me feel I am doing something, that's the most important thing."

"Teaching should be just the job for that feeling," the priest said.

"But it's so far away and everything," Ken said. "You can't see that you're doing anything."

"But you should know you are even if you can't see it."

"I know that, but—well, I don't know."

"We can talk about that later," the priest said. "The important thing now is to get you a job." The cigarette hadn't been out of his mouth since it was made, and now the long ash broke off with the motion of his lips and dribbled over the front of his robe. "It isn't going to be as easy now as it looks. How old are you?"

"Twenty-three, father."

"What about the draft?"

"I got a deferment because the school board cried so loud about losing all their men teachers, but I guess my chances of deferment are about as good in the shipyard."

"Mmm." And the cigarette came out of his mouth now and was jabbed fiery-pointing at Ken. "But I want you in the meantime to be thinking that the teacher who stays in there day after day and gives the best he's got is doing more for the war effort and the next war and the peace too than any war worker can ever do. And don't forget the work of God he can be doing too. I don't mean propaganda. I mean just being a good Catholic and living a good Catholic life. Twenty-three is barely young enough, but it will do. Here, I'll give you a note." He tore a page from a pocket notebook, also from the depths of his robe, and wrote, squinting through the smoke rising in his face from the cigarette now back in his mouth.

"Thank you, father," Ken said. He took the note and held it in his fist on the table.

"Now, this is to the director of the NYA trade school," the priest said. "They're training welders now. This isn't really a job, but in a couple of weeks you should be able to learn enough to go out to the shipyards and get a job."

"Yes, father."

"Go out to the shipyards as soon as you can. Don't wait until they think you're ready. It's just like any other school. It can't teach you anything. You have to learn it on the job, right?"

"Right, father."

"What did your college of education teach you about teaching? Confess now. Nothing, right?"

"Right, father."

The tobacco sack was again dangling under the priest's chin. "So you pick up what you can in a couple of weeks and go out to the shipyards, OK?"

"OK, father."

The priest scratched his match on the sole of his shoe and stood up lighting his cigarette. "If you need money to tide you over while you're going to school, we'll see what we can do."

"I'll be all right, father."

"Good," the priest said and battered him on the shoulder and steered him to the door.

As they were standing in the doorway, an old crone scuttled down the alley and, throwing a shawl over her hair, entered the side door of the cathedral. "Aha," the priest said, "have you made your Easter duty?"

And Ken said, "No, father." Everything had gone so well up until then that for a moment he got careless and told a needless truth. He didn't add, however, that it had been some years since he made an Easter duty.

"It's a good thing I thought of it," the priest said. "Tomorrow will be the last day, you know."

"Indeed, father? I had forgotten."

"Father Staedtler is hearing confessions now, so you'd better run over and get it done before you forget again."

"Thank you, father, for reminding me," Ken said. "I wouldn't want to forget."

"Mortal sin," the priest said.

"Yes, father," Ken said. He crossed the alley to the side door of the cathedral. As he turned to open the door, he saw out of the corner of his eye that Father Van was still standing in the doorway watching him.

Then he was in the church, quiet and dim and holy. The votive lights flickered in banks along the altar, and the vigil light shone dull red as it always had in every church he had ever seen. He thought for a moment he could smell incense. His ears throbbed and hummed in the quilted silence. His steps were sharp in the empty church. And it was all as if he had never been away.

He saw the old woman with the shawl just entering the confessional, and he tiptoed toward the place, dipping his fingers in holy water and blessing himself as he went. He didn't even have to think about any of it, but when he genuflected before entering a pew, his knee thudded loud on the floor. Again he blessed himself and knelt and began to say prayers he would have sworn he had forgotten. But when he tried to examine his conscience, he found that he had no conscience. He was aware that he had broken most of the commandments a man was likely to have any occasion to break. Those he had had no occasion to break he hadn't broken. No murder, for instance. No worshiping of strange gods. No marrying within the fourth degree of kindred.

Everything had come back so easily that he was afraid for a moment that in spite of himself he would confess everything and wind up with a penance that would take him all night to do so that he wouldn't have a chance to get back and thank that Walker girl, who had begun to grow on him now that he suddenly thought of her. So it was reassuring to discover that he didn't have a conscience to trip him up and maybe lose him the job if the word or even the hint of what he had done ever got back to Father Van because a man with a conscience would surely have to confess that.

Then he carefully worked out a list of sins for a moderately good man who had last been to confession six months ago.

When the old woman at last came out of the confessional, he went in and knelt in the dark behind the curtain. He felt with his fingertips the wire mesh before his face, and he heard the priest open and close the slide on the other side of the confessional. Evidently no one was there. Then the slide in front of him opened, and he could see the white blur of the priest's profile and his white hand moving in the dark. In the instant that the hand was moving in the sign of the cross, he thought in panic that he had forgotten what he had to say, but when the priest inclined his head on his hand and blotted out his profile and showed only his ear, Ken heard himself say, "Bless me, father, for I have sinned."

Since no priest was ever going to believe the record of his life, dull as it was, and since he wasn't bound by any actuality, he gave himself credit for the normal vices one would expect of a man of his age living alone in New Orleans. Immoderation in drink: every Saturday. Bad women: every Saturday and some Wednesdays. Swearing: a dozen times a day. Missing mass: twice in the six months. Lying: only when necessary.

For his penance he got five Hail Marys and five Our Fathers, just what he used to get when he made his monthly confession for the boys' Sunday. Only then it had been sassing mother, once, cussing (cheese and rice), twice, impure thoughts, sometimes.

He did his penance directly in front of the statue of the Sacred Heart, and it never moved or changed expression any more than it had in those other days when, praying fervently and ticking off the prayers on his fingers under cover of the altar rail and feeling the sins drop off him one by one as he prayed, he had waited, feeling lighter and lighter and higher and holier all the time, for it to move or smile. When he left the cathedral, he left by the front door and walked home through Pirates' Alley although it was a little longer that way.

When he got back to the house he found a note from Alice (a disappointment and a relief) explaining that she had waited as long as she dared before going to work. She asked him to let her know how he made out with Father Van. This note and the priest's note he taped to the mirror in the bathroom where he'd be sure to find them first thing in the morning. Then he sat down in his doorway.

He flipped one cigarette after another toward the invisible

fountain that now at night seemed to flow again in the liquid rustle of banana leaves, but other than that he didn't hear much of anything.

An orchestra was playing at a patio restaurant at the other end of the block. Just outside his own patio gate a couple stopped to whisper in the shadow of the banana leaves—he knew the spot—one laughing softly yes, the other, no. A torrential argument in French drowned all other sound for a time and then subsided. People were praying together, perhaps where the corpse was laid out. A bed was banging against a wall. The mailbox at the corner clanged sharply as someone made sure a letter was mailed. In moments of greatest silence he could hear the creaking of the rocking chair where the old man sat in the floor-length window listening—rocking, smoking his pipe, and listening.

And though the night drifted beyond midnight, Ken still didn't go to bed to get the rest he knew he ought to have for a new job. He kept on listening while sounds went under one by one until there was only the hum of insects, the rattle of distant street cars, and the whistling of ships on the river—these and the hidden shouts of sleepers, which let him hear as well his own blood tapping at his ears.

Then at last he went to bed but didn't sleep until just about cockcrow, just about daybreak.

The Bribe

Driving four children to and from school had seemed to John Roberts an easy way to make money. When an old service buddy who had started a private school and who threw the school's legal business his way consulted him about the law governing school buses, John Roberts quoted the law and offered himself as a reliable driver for, strangely enough, the figure mentioned coincided almost exactly with the monthly payments on the car he felt his position required but could not yet support. He also felt that it would be pleasant to get into his new car and drive around the city twice a day with nothing on his mind.

All that was before he met Elly, John, Sophie and Florence. All that was before he discovered that John Roberts did not take little rides in his car but that a Mr. Roberts was engaged in the business of transporting children. He didn't know precisely when he discovered it, but he had discovered it by the first of December. It was disconcerting.

Mr. Roberts stopped the car in front of Sophie's house. He blew the horn. He sighed and switched off the engine. No matter what time he got to Sophie's he had to wait ten to fifteen minutes for her to get ready. He slumped in his seat and tried to project a feeling of relaxed patience through the car. Already the two children in the back seat were grumbling, and Elly, by far the youngest of the children, was bouncing on the seat beside him.

"Why don't we just go and leave Sophie?" Florence said, leaning over the back of the seat.

"It would be a good idea," Mr. Roberts said, "but we just can't do it." He wondered why they just couldn't. It was a simple matter of starting the car and driving away. But he couldn't. Sometime—soon—he would issue an ultimatum: ready or else. But he couldn't —not now.

He sighed and picked up his paper from the seat beside him. The paper was limp in his hands and dirty like a paper picked up from the subway floor. It had been crisp and fresh when he picked it out of the rosebush beside his front steps. He had put it neatly on the seat of the car and had pleasantly contemplated reading it, perhaps at Sophie's, perhaps with his coffee before he took the elevator up to his office. But now the paper was scuffed and worn. "Elly," Mr. Roberts said, "Elly, in heaven's name—" But as the small dark head turned from the window and the doe eyes focused full on him, he knew there was nothing to say to Elly. He was not even sure she spoke English. He did not understand the patois of the nursery school.

Every morning Elly climbed onto the seat and jumped up and down shouting, "junkin jack, junkin jack," which she certainly was: she junked his paper regularly, she had junked the radio once and the clock twice; the heater seemed indestructible although she had attacked it with pliers and a screw driver from the glove compartment. And each time he spoke to her she looked on him with the mild eyes of the first fawn after the creation of the world.

"Elly," Florence said. Mr. Roberts turned to his paper and left Elly to Florence. Florence leaned over the back of the seat and took up the discipline which she had assumed from the first day they all rode to school with Mr. Roberts. Florence was much older than the others. She was almost, though not quite, a young lady. She maintained a highhanded discipline with threats, cajolery, a weekly prize for conduct and occasional physical force. All of this so fascinated Mr. Roberts—to say nothing of relieving him of the responsibility of keeping order—that he gave his tacit consent and watched with never-ending wonder the workings of a microcosmic morality.

"Elly," Florence said, "what have you done now?"

"She hasn't done anything, bossy," John said.

"You keep out of this, John Bellamy," Florence said, "and mind your own business."

"It's my business as much as yours," John said. "I don't have to take orders from you."

"I'm the oldest in this car and what I say goes," Florence said.

"You are not either the oldest," John said.

"Except for Mr. Roberts." Over the top of his newspaper, in the mirror, Mr. Roberts saw Florence gave a brisk nod toward him without taking her eyes off John.

"All right, then you aren't the oldest. The only one I have to take orders from in this car is Mr. Roberts."

"I'm the oldest of the children," Florence said, "and I say sit down and shut up."

"I don't have to take orders from you," John said. He sat down and was quiet.

"That's better. I didn't want to have to sit on you," Florence said. The *peine forte et dure* was one of Florence's specialties. Her vastly superior size made it easy for her to sit on the others and impress on them in that way her idea of what was right and just. She sat on the children in the back seat with all the vigorous righteousness of Judge Hathorne pressing to death poor Giles Corey at Salem.

Out of the corner of his eye Mr. Roberts saw the door of Sophie's house open. He turned to watch Sophie mince down the path. Because he knew that Sophie minced she appeared to mince, although actually she clumped heavily in her mother's stadium boots. He opened the door and called, "Hurry, Sophie."

Sophie stopped halfway down the path and turned and walked back to the house. At the door she screamed, "I hate this old scarf." She tore the scarf from her head. The door opened and a faded Paisley scarf was shaken forth. Sophie snatched it, dropping the bright plaid on the steps. Tying the Paisley around her head, she walked to the car and got in.

"Good morning, Sophie," Mr. Roberts said.

"Good morning," Sophie said. She sat down beside John and folded her hands demurely in her lap.

"John," Florence said, "move over into the other corner. I'm going to sit between you two today."

"She's my old girl friend," John said. "I have to sit next to her."

"Into the corner." John moved. "Now," Florence said, settling herself in the middle of the seat, "we'll have no more of that disgusting kissing." John looked out of the window casually. Was it possible, Mr. Roberts thought, that in the mirror Sophie's demureness darkened almost imperceptibly?

The remainder of the trip was uneventful. Once John leaned over the back of the seat and said, "Why do you have the mirror fixed like that? All I can see is trees."

Mr. Roberts drew back from the very brink of an abysmal discussion of angles of incidence and reflection. He congratulated himself on his new found craftiness. He shudderingly remembered his learned discourse on why he had chains on his car while John's father didn't. "I like to look at trees," he said.

"That's crazy," John said.

But they were at school and Mr. Roberts felt he had got through the morning trip with remarkably little damage to his sanity.

There were two things that made the next week different from all the other weeks during which Mr. Roberts had driven the children to school. One morning Mr. Roberts drove up to Sophie's house to find her standing at the end of the walk.

"My mother went to Chicago," Sophie said as she got in. That was all she said, and for a week every morning she was standing at the end of the walk when Mr. Roberts drove up. In the afternoon she got out of the car as soon as it stopped. Ordinarily she got down in a corner and refused to get out until Mr. Roberts picked her up and carried her, shrieking with laughter, to the door—except on the days (very infrequent days) she saw her mother's car in the driveway; on those days she got directly out and ran into the house.

Mr. Roberts felt he was making a mistake to take part in her game in the afternoon and to wait for her in the morning, but he didn't know what else to do. If Sophie were a case history in a textbook—Mr. Roberts had become interested in child psychology although none of the standard cases ever came up in the car—he would be able to follow the unfolding of the difficulty and the correction. But Sophie was not a textbook case; she was a real little girl who was late in the morning and reluctant in the afternoon, and there was no professor pointing out cause and cure.

The second thing that made that week different from all the others was Florence's illness. One afternoon Mr. Roberts got to the school and was told that Florence had been taken home ill. She was out the whole week. And it was Florence's absence that had the most far-reaching influence on the character of the week. There was the simple matter of conduct in the car. For example:

All three children sat in the back seat. John was repeatedly embracing Sophie with more determination than real interest. Sophie stared blankly away or perhaps turned her head aside from John although even then her face revealed no emotion. Mr. Roberts was passing the time of day with himself wondering idly about the relations of John's father with his wife and of Sophie's mother with her husband and what could be deduced from the observation of the children's pattern of erotic behavior, when some part of his mind became aware of a low chant that Elly had been carrying on. He didn't know when it had started, but it was low, slow and monotonous, as if it had been going on from primitive time. "Arrah barrah boosah, arrah barrah boosah," she crooned endlessly.

"Ella bella broomstick, yourself," John shouted. He was evidently pleased with himself. "Ella bella broomstick," he repeated laughing.

Sophie laughed too. "Ella bella broomstick," she said. She repeated it with John joining in. And again with John and Elly. From then it was endless, first one and then the other shrieking the words while the other two kept up an accompaniment that increased in tempo imperceptibly but relentlessly. In the mirror Mr. Roberts could see their glazed eyes and wooden faces. He was fascinated.

The syllables had degenerated again to arrah barrah boosah and went on and on. Mr. Roberts concentrated on his driving while the

chant swept around him. Dimly, but without surprise, he felt himself clutching the wheel and growling in his throat, "Arrah barrah
boosah." He shook the wheel and growled.

The screech of brakes brought him to his senses. He had a brief
view of a truck and a brandished fist, and he knew he had gone
through a red light. Trembling, he pulled over to the curb and
stopped, rather more roughly than necessary. The sudden stop piled
the children on the floor.

"What's the idea?" John said.

"We almost hit a truck," Mr. Roberts said. Elly was sniffling
a little. Sophie smoothed her dress meticulously. Aside from the
mere matter of discipline, Florence's absence had one other effect:
Mr. Roberts found himself with a full-scale conspiracy and rebellion
on his hands. Fortunately, the rebellion was not aimed against him
and, even more fortunately, the suppressed fury of the conspiracy
was an endless drain on the energies of the children. They were
abnormally well-behaved except that their whispered talk bristled
with manifestoes, violence and poisons.

On the very morning of Florence's absence it began. "Elly,
Sophie," John said, "listen to me. Now that Florence is sick we can
do what we please—except, of course, what Mr. Roberts tells us not
to." He nodded toward Mr. Roberts, who inclined his head gra-
ciously. "And the first thing we've got to do is make sure we can
always do what we want."

"She's too bossy," Sophie said.

"I'll bring a saw and saw her head off," Elly said.

"The first thing we've got to do is write a letter to Florence.
We'll give it to her as soon as she gets in the car. We'll tell her she's
too bossy and we don't have to do what she says. You write the
letter, Sophie, and we'll all sign it."

Sophie said, "I'll say, 'Dear Florence, You are too bossy. We
hate you.' "

"Stuff like that," John said. "I'll take care of the poison."

"Poison!" Sophie said.

"I'll bring a meat grinder and grind up her nose," Elly said.

"Real poison," John said, lowering his voice to a subdued shout. "I've got some rat poison, the rat. And I'll mix it with castor oil and chemicals my father uses in his darkroom, and I'll color it with my mother's coloring, and flavor it with her flavoring, and I'll put it in a Coke bottle, and I'll say, 'Look at this nice Coke, Florence,' and she'll drink it, and then we can always do what we want."

"And I'll write the letter," Sophie said, "and she'll read it, and she'll be mad, but she can't do anything."

"Good," John said. "You take care of the letter and I'll take care of the poison. And Elly, are you on our side?"

"OK," Elly said.

"Good," John said. "If we all stick together, I'll fix that Florence."

That morning when Mr. Roberts stopped for a tonic for his nerves, he casually invited the bartender to join him and surreptitiously watched him take the first drink.

At the beginning of the next week Florence came back, and when they got to Sophie's house they had to wait. "Her mother must be back," John said.

Sophie came out at last. "My mother is back," she said.

"Have you got it?" John said.

"Yes," Sophie said. "Have you got it?"

"No," John said. "I couldn't get the chemicals. Give her yours."

Sophie brought a crumpled piece of composition paper out of her snow suit. "For you," she said giving it to Florence.

"My, what can this be?" Florence said. She laughed. She was in rare good humor and very frisky, like a colt out of the stable in springtime. She had even pulled Mr. Roberts' hat down over his eyes, a thing she was constantly punishing the others for. It was a major crime in her book and she gave extra bounces when she sat on the culprit.

"Read it," John said.

"You'll see," Sophie said.

"I'll bring a hammer and pound nails in her eyes," Elly said.

"Well, I must say," Florence said. "This isn't very nice. Who wrote it?"

"We all signed it," John said. He twisted around and pointed to the bottom of the note. "This X is for Elly."

"Why, Elly, I thought you were on my side," Florence said. "After all the bubble gum I gave you."

"Bubble gum," Elly said.

"If you promise never to do such a thing again," Florence said, "I'll give you a piece of bubble gum. Promise?"

"Give?"

"Here."

"Promise."

"All right for you, Elly," John said. "You're still on my side, aren't you, Sophie?"

Sophie didn't say yes, but neither did she say no when John put his arm around her.

"And, by the way," Florence said, "you spell *orders* o-R-d-e-r-s, and *Florence* with a *c,* not an *s.*" She folded the note carefully and put it in one of her books.

Clearly, Florence had won at least a partial victory. Mr. Roberts rather regretted Elly's easy duplicity, but she was, he supposed, too young to have developed a moral sense. Group loyalty and personal integrity would come later. As it was, she represented a very early stage of social evolution, a stage still manifested by small children who have not completely evolved, and by people like Nazis who have regressed.

"All right," Florence said, "none of that kissing."

"Try and stop me," John said. He sprang from the seat and braced his back against the door. (Mr. Roberts felt hastily to make sure the door was locked.) He moved his hands and one foot defensively before him, making himself rather a thorny object there in cramped quarters.

"You asked for it." Florence began to move cautiously toward him.

"You leave him alone," Sophie shrieked. She pranced on the seat beside Florence, her hands extended like claws.

Florence backed off a little to get both John and Sophie in front of her. They all hung in equilibrium between fear and regret. They all were on the defensive. They all lacked diplomacy to avoid violence and yet save face. Mr. Roberts, in spite of the tension and unpleasantness, was gratified that Sophie should stand by John and her own principles, and even the principles of civilization.

"Here we are at school," Mr. Roberts said. "Everyone sit down while we turn into the drive."

They all sat down. It was the one thing he said they always paid attention to. After each of them had fallen and cried when they bumped up over the sidewalk, they sat down when he turned into the drive: they could at least learn to respect the laws of physics, if not the conventions of morality.

When the children got into the car that afternoon, Mr. Roberts began to wonder if he had perhaps misunderstood what had happened in the morning. It had seemed to him that a stalemate had been reached, that the locations of power had been thrown into flux and had, at least for the time being, arrived at a new uneasy equilibrium, with Florence being forced to give up much of her power to the John-Sophie coalition but still retaining enough to keep them inactive. However, that was certainly not the way John and Sophie viewed it. They got into the car first.

"I guess we showed that Florence," John said.

"We sure did," Sophie said.

"I guess we can do what we want now," John said.

"We sure can," Sophie said.

"Keep your feet off the seat," Mr. Roberts said.

"OK," John said.

"OK," Sophie said.

"We'll make her sit in front with Mr. Roberts," John said.

"And we won't let her turn around," Sophie said.

Florence stepped to the car door and began to get in with her customary air of authority. John and Sophie hesitated and were lost. "Get in front," John said gruffly.

"There's no room here," Sophie said.

By then Florence was seated. She laughed briefly her hoarse, cackling laugh and taking Elly on her lap began to tell her the story of Br'er Rabbit and the Forty Thieves. John glared at her although she was blandly unaware of him. He turned from her and threw himself on Sophie, embracing her brutally. Outside of adjusting her balance, Sophie made no response.

"Here now," Florence said, "none of that."

John sprang up and braced himself against the door, snarling. "I'd like to see you stop me," he shouted. "My mother says you're too bossy."

In her lap Sophie's demure hands tensed and tightened. Her fingers hooked and spread. Her eyes were veiled by drooping lashes.

Mr. Roberts prepared for a crash stop to throw all the children in a pile if worst came to worst.

But Florence was quite unmoved. "I think you'll stop," she said.

John relaxed a little. He began to appear apprehensively curious. Sophie's eyes remained veiled and her fingers hid themselves in each other.

"You two are in Miss Johnson's room, aren't you?" Florence said.

"What of it?" John said. Even Mr. Roberts began to be a little apprehensive.

"Well," Florence said casually, "suppose I told Miss Johnson that you two wrote a letter to me and called me filthy names and said nasty things about me and threatened to poison me."

"She wouldn't believe you," John said.

"Suppose I showed her the letter," Florence said.

"Come on, Soph," John said, "we've got to get that letter." He began to move toward Florence.

Florence's cackling laugh stopped him. "Do you think I'd carry it with me?" she said. "I hid it in school."

"So what?" John said.

"So I called my father on the telephone—he's a lawyer and so is your father, Sophie, so you should have known this—and he says that it's a criminal offense to write a threatening letter. You can be put in jail for it."

"Is that right, Sophie?" John said.

"I think it is," Sophie said. She began to cry.

"Of course, I haven't told Miss Johnson," Florence said, "and I hope I don't have to, but if I have to, I will."

Sophie cried louder. John absently slipped his arm around her and patted her shoulder. "There, there," he said. He stared bleakly before him like a man who sees nothing ahead but years of tension and shame and insecurity under the dark shadow of blackmail.

It was blackmail, Mr. Roberts realized with a start, nothing but blackmail.

"Don't cry, Sophie," Florence said, "probably nothing will ever come of it—*probably*. How would you like to ask your mother if you can come over to my house this afternoon? I'll help you with your arithmetic, and we'll make tea with my old doll's set I've still got around somewhere."

Sophie stopped crying at once. "Mr. Roberts, will you wait for me?" she said.

By then they were at Sophie's house. "Of course," Mr. Roberts said automatically, "but hurry." He slumped down in his seat. He was upset by Sophie's abandonment of her common cause with John. Now John was alone. It wasn't so bad for Elly. She was too little to know. But Sophie—was she perhaps eight?—surely must have some concept of right and wrong and loyalty and honor.

Clearly, that lack of personal integrity was even more disturbing than Florence's brazen attempt at blackmail.

Mr. Roberts was quite disappointed in Sophie. It was true that she displayed considerable lack of consideration of others by making them all wait in the morning. And now on top of her perfidy she was making them wait in the afternoon. It was too much entirely. Some things are not to be borne. In the morning he would issue an ultimatum: ready or else. The time had clearly come. He could do it now.

John stood up as if to get out of the car. "Sit down," Florence said.

"Try and make me," John said. He stopped in the doorway.

"Sit down and shut up," Florence said. She spoke softly and smiled gently.

"I don't have to take orders from you," John said. He sat down and was quiet.

Sophie minced down the walk carrying a gift-wrapped package. As she got in she handed it to Mr. Roberts. Speaking rapidly as if to avoid forgetting she said, "My mother says to thank you for waiting for me all the time. She says she doesn't know what she would have done without you. And I will try to be better from now on." She sat down beside Florence.

Mr. Roberts took the package automatically. It was heavy in his hand. He smiled at Sophie's anticipation of his smile. He said thank you when she had finished. As he held the package and shook it, the liquor laughed softly in his ear, and he knew there would be no ultimatum.

A Spring

It wasn't at all as I had planned. The Chicken Shack was, I now saw, grimy and ordinary, but we were too hungry and tired to drive on farther, so we sat down at the booth in the corner, the only booth where the table wasn't covered with empty beer bottles and glasses and spilled beer and crumpled cellophane and ashes. I began to think as we sat, Ruth and I together, and Andre opposite, waiting to be noticed, that what I had learned and wanted to show about the South wouldn't come through any better here than it had all day at the plantation houses we had visited and the mill towns we had seen. I began to think that we might have eaten anywhere along the way and not waited until we reached this place; this place I remembered so fondly from my undergraduate days that even as I sat uneasily in the booth I fancied I recognized the big M carved into the blackened wood of the table top.

As I looked around the Shack I saw how foolish I had been to insist that we ride on so long after we were hungry. But the whole day had been like that. Nothing worked out well. It was all disorganized despite the fact that we had always intended to take Andre down through the Black Belt to see the spring. Somehow spring came that year and almost went before we realized it. Even then we wouldn't have gone if Andre hadn't received orders to return to France. So we suddenly picked up and went on a day we hadn't chosen to see a spring that was almost past.

Magnolias were everywhere past their firmness and hung flabby, waiting for the death by the night wind, but at the last house we visited, a house where I had long ago been introduced by Southerners, where I had my visa stamped, a vouched-for foreigner —at that house an old gentleman in broken tennis shoes and rumpled khakis gave Andre a magnolia to take with him. We had brought the old gentleman a pint of whiskey as protocol demanded and had at his insistence accepted his hospitality, sitting in the twilight on the sagging veranda with our backs to the house, passing the bottle from hand to hand until it was empty. He gave us the magnolia, the best of the lot, to take with us from his land. Andre still held it cupped in his hands when we got to the Chicken Shack.

This last house, then, was my one triumph of the day, but as I thought about it there in the Shack I felt not triumph but depression: I had indeed shown that I knew something but not even I knew what it was.

Just as it seemed no one was going to take our order, the bartender came out from behind the bar and stood beside the table, his hands on his hips. "Chicken, folks?" he said. "That's all they is."

"How come the dining room's closed?" I said.

"Nobody travelling these days," the bartender said. "Not enough university boys get down this way now to pay to keep any girls around."

Ruth took a paper napkin and began to scrub the table. "Crumbs," she said, "look at them." The bartender turned and took a cloth from the bar and wiped the table casually, leaving it streaked with water. Ruth carefully dried the space in front of her. Andre smiled broadly as he always did when the conversation was too fast or too colloquial for him to follow.

Ruth started to dry the space in front of me. "Aren't you going to order?" she said.

"What do you want?" I said.

"Chicken, of course. What else is there?"

"Chicken for all of us," I said.

"Was that so hard?" Ruth said. "Was it so hard to make up your mind to order the only thing they had?"

"No," I said.

"And you forgot to order beer," she said.

I said, "For god's sake don't crowd me. Three beers," I called to the bartender, who was just coming out of the kitchen. He set the opened bottles on the bar with the tumblers inverted over them. I went to the bar and brought the beer to the table. Although Ruth said nothing further I knew that she felt I had let her down by not being masterful in ordering the chicken and handling the bartender. I sipped my beer and began to hope as I usually do under such circumstances that a good meal would straighten everything out.

We had drunk two bottles of beer and the bartender was just setting our basket of chicken on the table when Lt. de Clermont walked in. Andre sprang to his feet. Lt. de Clermont waved a deprecating hand and went to a table at the other end of the room and sat down. Andre sat down and leaned across the table toward us and said, "That is Lt. de Clermont." We nodded. "Lt. de Clermont is my commanding officer," Andre said, enunciating each word carefully. "Lt. de Clermont is an important man."

"Really?" Ruth said.

Andre spoke seriously but he was grinning over his success in English. "Yes, Ruth," he said, "before the occupation Lt. de Clermont was one of the biggest aces in France."

"Really?" I said. I stole a quick glance across the room to where Lt. de Clermont sat alone. He was a very thin man, small and of extremely formal carriage. As I watched him ask for a menu and then order his chicken in a faultless English that the bartender had difficulty understanding, I was impressed by his reserve, his gravity, his melancholy. He wasn't at all what I would have expected an ace to be.

"But why didn't you invite him to sit at our table?" Ruth said.

"Oh, no," Andre said. "I could not do that. He is de Clermont. Nobility. Power. Money. He is related to the greatest families of France."

"But—" Ruth said. I kicked her under the table, for where

liberty, equality, and fraternity are concerned Ruth has no discretion whatever. "But," she said again, this time in a modulated tone I was willing to let pass, "aren't you both officers? Aren't you the only two French officers at the field and shouldn't you be social equals?"

"You are Americans," Andre said. He smiled tolerantly. "We French are different."

"It is very strange," Ruth said, lapsing into the strangely formal English we ordinarily spoke to Andre.

"Oui, c'est étrange," I said in the strange French which was our last desperate means of communication.

"Yes, Ruth, oui, Mike," Andre said, "c'est strange." Yet we shouldn't have been surprised at this attitude in Andre. His sense of propriety was staggering. He was outraged, for example, if he heard a student yell at me on campus, and once when he was cooking a French meal for us, we had to pull down all the shades in the house before he would put on an apron to protect his uniform: some of his cadets might see him in an undignified position, he said; it would be bad for discipline. We began our chicken in silence, looking away from the table for something to talk about.

There was a grizzled ragged man asleep in one of the booths, but none of us seemed to have anything to say about him. A truck driver came in and got change for fifty cents to call Bloomberg. He walked back to the phone booth, which was barricaded with cases of beer, and brought the bartender the phone book. The bartender looked through the dirty pages and told him the number. When the truck driver had closed himself into the booth, everything was motionless again, so I set the bartender moving by holding up my empty beer bottle. We watched him get the bottles and bring them to us as if we had never seen a bartender or a bottle of beer, and then we poured the beer and watched it foam and tasted it and nodded our heads approvingly as if it were all strange and new.

The truck driver came back and I nodded my head toward him

as much as to say to Ruth and Andre that the comedy was about to begin although actually I had little confidence. They both looked around and watched the bartender and the truck driver settle themselves at one end of the bar with a newspaper spread out before them. "He says to wait," the truck driver said. Ruth and Andre didn't seem to be much interested: she was still a little belligerent, and he was looking here, there, and everywhere and smiling all the time. Lt. de Clermont, I could see out of the corner of my eye, was eating carefully and slowly and watching the men at the bar and us impartially. The fact that we were eating the chicken with our fingers seemed to interest him no less than the fact that the bartender and the truck driver passed a pair of glasses back and forth while they bent over their paper.

"The weight and distance is right," the truck driver said.

"Here, let me see," the bartender said. He took the glasses and held them to his eyes. The forefinger of his other hand moved thickly across the page while his lips smacked over the words. "Unless the track is muddy," he said.

A young man came in and stood at the bar. "A beer," he called.

The truck driver took the glasses. "Fair and warm," he said.

The bartender held the glasses up to his eyes. "They've been having rain to the west," he said, squinting at the top of the west wall. He passed the glasses to the truck driver and walked around behind the bar.

The bartender set up the beer for the young man, who leaned forward and spoke into the dead quiet with the casual tone of a man who has just thought of something of no great importance. "Are there any cabins left?" the young man said.

"Yes, indeed," the bartender said clear and very loud.

"I'd like to pay now," the young man said.

"Good." The bartender took the bill and picked up a key and a flashlight from the counter near the cash register. (He put the bill in his pocket.) As the young man turned from the bar he looked very briefly at me. I stared through him and froze my face until he had finished his turn. The bartender led the way out the door. The young man hadn't touched his beer. The truck driver sat hunched over the paper, poking at it with the stub of a pencil.

We had all watched the bartender and the young man go out the door, and as we turned back to the table our eyes met for the first time. I looked away quickly, reluctant to take up conversation at that precise point, and saw Lt. de Clermont's eyes, still swinging slowly from the door, pause briefly on us, pause briefly on the truck driver, and pass on to his plate. Ruth, because of five years of marriage and two children, was altogether too naive to know what was happening. Andre's inadequate English kept him from knowing. The truck driver was obviously casehardened. Only Lt. de Clermont and I had seen everything and understood everything, yet in the moment when our eyes met he showed nothing. It came to me suddenly that while I had been watching the young man, Lt. de Clermont had not only been watching the young man, but had also been watching me watching the young man.

"This is your spring?" Andre said, suddenly breaking into the conversation I had been putting off. "These houses? These people?"

"These people. This cotton," Ruth said. "These dairy farms. This magnolia." She held it up but it was already the color of tobacco.

"Oh," Andre said, "how it is too bad. I meant to sit and look at it and write my wife in Algiers about the spring and this day and you, my friends. And now it will be difficult to remember just how it was."

Again I looked away from the table and again I met Lt. de Clermont's unembarrassed eye. I turned my head casually toward the bar, but I could tell that Lt. de Clermont between bites continued to regard us and the men at the bar impartially. When I had prepared a face to turn toward Andre, I saw that he was chewing happily with his customary expression of delighted bewilderment spread up over his face. Ruth was digging furiously in her purse. "Cigarette," she said. Andre had his cigarettes out and her cigarette lighted before I could get the cellophane off a fresh pack. I crumpled the cellophane into a tight wad and put it in the ash tray where it writhed slowly with soft crackling as it opened out again.

The bartender brought us another round of beer. "He says he wishes you have a good appetite," the bartender said, jerking his head toward Lt. de Clermont. I raised my glass toward the lieutenant. Ruth and Andre raised their glasses. Unsmiling the lieutenant bowed and raised his glass to us and then bowed and raised his glass to the bartender and the truck driver, who nodded curtly to him and turned at once back to their paper. Their heads leaned together. They passed the glasses back and forth and scribbled on the margin of the page.

We were finishing our chicken and it was almost time to say something about what we had seen during the day. I couldn't put it off much longer. I had no idea what could be said, but I was beginning to believe as we ate the good chicken and sat comfortably that our talk and our memories of the day would somehow be shaped into the pattern of what I had originally intended the day to be and mean.

I was just getting ready to start talking, not about anything, just talking because I know that a lot of the time if I can only start I'll say something before I'm done. As I was trying to think how to begin, a Negro came in through the kitchen door. He was covered from chin to ankles in a dirty white apron that went around him nearly twice. On his head he wore a woman's stocking, knotted and the foot cut off. He stood beside the bar waiting to be noticed. He moved restlessly, making small sounds with his feet and breathing heavily. The bartender didn't look up.

I lit a cigarette and choked on the smoke. The bartender didn't look up. I tossed off the beer Lt. de Clermont had sent over. "Another beer," I called.

"Take it easy," Ruth said.

"I know what I'm doing," I said.

"Oh, fine," she said. "That's a sure sign. I didn't think you were that bad already."

"We'll carry him home like a little *bébé* and put him to bed," Andre said, cradling his arms and pretending to rock a baby. I could gladly have shot him, for Ruth needs no help when it comes to what she calls my drinking. She is convinced even after five years that I will at any moment revert to what she fondly believes were my bachelor habits.

After the bartender brought me the beer, he walked over to the Negro. "What do you want in here?" he said. I sat back to watch what I had set in motion. I glanced over to see if Lt. de Clermont was watching too, and he wasn't: he was watching me. That brought me up short. Clearly he was expecting something further from me, and I wondered if after all I had known what I was doing.

"A bottle of beer, please, sir," the Negro said. "I got a dollar."

"Let me see it," the bartender said. He leaned on the bar and studied the dollar. "Where'd you get this?"

"The young fella gave it to me for more towels," the Negro said.

"She bleed?" the bartender said, smiling. When he began to smile I relaxed. I relaxed so completely that I quite forgot to notice how Ruth was reacting. Andre, I could see without turning, was smiling broadly, but I was certain he didn't have the least idea what was being said. I was startled, however, to observe that Lt. de Clermont became more interested as I relaxed my interest. He stopped eating and leaned forward although he persisted in staring at me rather than at the Negro.

The Negro laughed. "Like a pig," he said.

"Well, I'm glad you've got this dollar," the bartender said. "I'm glad you want to treat me and Sam to a drink. That shows a lot of friendliness. Don't you call that friendly, Sam?" I began to get a little uneasy.

"Yes, indeed," the truck driver said, "real friendly. I like a friendly nigra."

"So do I," the bartender said, "and I think we should let him sit at the bar to show we're friendly too." I was decidedly uneasy for there was nothing friendly in his voice.

"Good idea," the truck driver said. The Negro moved cautiously toward a bar stool.

"Not on the stool," the bartender said. "It doesn't have a back. Go in the other room and take a chair from one of the tables."

The Negro brought back a low straight chair of no grace or comfort. He set it before the bar and sat down. The bartender and the truck driver were sipping their beer. "Thank you for the beer," the truck driver said. "Here's to you."

"Yes, here's to you," the bartender said. "But you should come up here where we can see you. All we can see is the top of your head."

The Negro stood up. "No, no," the truck driver said. "Sit down, be comfortable. We only want to be sure you're enjoying this as much as we are."

The Negro crouched over the chair and extended his neck. "That's better," the bartender said. "We can't be sure unless we see your smiling face." The Negro smiled miserably.

He was the only one in the room who smiled at all. The bartender and the truck driver had gone back to their paper. Lt. de Clermont was detached and impassive as always. Ruth was staring slack-jawed.

Even Andre had stopped smiling. "How can they do this?" he said. "It is indecent."

"Could I at least have my beer, please, sir?" the Negro said.

"At least?" the truck driver said.

"At this fine party he says at least," the bartender said. He shook his head gently. "Now how about cigars? You wouldn't expect us to really enjoy our beer without a good cigar, would you?"

"Yes, sir," the Negro said, "you can't enjoy a beer without a good cigar."

"We thank you, sir," the truck driver said. He lit his cigar and held the light for the bartender.

"And I thank you both," the bartender said. "And now that you have relaxed and enjoyed our company, I'm sure that you'll want to entertain us with a dance."

"I don't know how to dance," the Negro said sullenly. He continued to smile with the perspiration streaming down his face and his whole body trembling from the strain of sitting without touching the chair.

"Why, all black people can dance," the truck driver said.

"It's how they show how happy they are," the bartender said. He had picked up the black bottle and fondled it absently as he spoke.

Ruth clutched my arm and whispered, "Do something, do something." I cleared my throat and raised my bottle toward the bartender, but he didn't see me. Andre snatched up an empty bottle and was half out of his seat when he instinctively glanced toward Lt. de Clermont and then sank back onto the bench. Lt. de Clermont had stopped watching. He was sitting back in his seat quietly lighting a cigarette. I was overcome with despair because I knew then that he foresaw the end and had lost interest. From the very beginning he had seen at least two moves further ahead than I did, and he was, now that he saw the end, no longer interested in what was going to happen to me.

The Negro began to dance. He shuffled and hopped and jigged on one foot.

Lt. de Clermont smoked his cigarette, looking straight ahead, lost in reverie. I jammed my hands into my pockets.

"I knew he was just bashful," the truck driver said.

"It's not a very happy dance," the bartender said. "Happier, man, happier." He picked up the glasses from the bar and studied the paper. "Look," he said. "Happy Man in the fifth. What could be more of a natural?" The truck driver took the glasses. The Negro began to hop faster, to wave his arms high over his head, and to show his teeth.

"Take it off!" The cry was thin and high and frantic. The grizzled, ragged man who had been asleep in one of the other booths when we came in was sitting up and staring wildly about. Again he shrieked, "Take it off!"

The Negro stopped dancing and turned and stared at the ragged man. The ragged man stared at the Negro. I almost held my breath with hope. I could feel Ruth's fingers move in my arm. Andre's mouth hung open just a little with concentration. Lt. de Clermont, after a single surprised glance at all of us, finished his glass of beer, savoring to the utmost the last half mouthful. Frantically I looked back at the ragged man.

"You heard the gentleman," the bartender said. "We're all friends here. Take it off. Dance." The Negro began to dance, fumbling at his apron strings. "Face us here," the bartender said. He walked around behind the Negro and picked up the dazed ragged man by the collar and the seat of the pants and threw him out the door. "The gentleman had to leave," he said, "but he wants you to go on dancing."

Hopping on one foot the Negro tugged at one of his old tennis shoes.

Ruth hid her face in my shoulder and her fingers relaxed. Andre closed his mouth and a little muscle danced under the white skin near his left eye. I saw with abnormal clarity that Ruth's cigarette had fallen off the ash tray and had burned almost its entire length along the table, leaving a long perfect ash on the surface of the wood. I saw that I was endlessly tracing with the beer bottle the carved M on the table before me.

Lt. de Clermont ground out his cigarette and stood up.

"Waiter," he said. I was half out of my seat before I realized that
the response wasn't mine to make. I could feel Ruth's fingers begin
ever so gently to move against my sleeve. "Waiter," Lt. de Clermont
said, and although I was prepared this time, all my muscles
twitched at the sound of his voice. "Waiter," he said, "my check."

The bartender slid around behind the cash register. "No
check," he said. "You owe me a dollar forty-five."

Lt. de Clermont laid a bill on the bar and counted out the balance coin by coin, a quarter and two dimes. We watched as atten-
tively as if he were conjuring the coins out of the air. "Good night,"
Lt. de Clermont said, turning from the bar.

"Good night," the bartender said.

"Good night," Lt. de Clermont said, nodding toward us.

Andre half rose, Ruth said nothing, I mumbled, "Good night."

When the door closed behind Lt. de Clermont, the truck driver
looked down at his paper, the bartender walked toward the truck
driver, the rest of us turned back toward where the Negro had
been. He had disappeared but neither the bartender nor the truck
driver seemed to notice.

We sat for a moment tensely, and at the sound of Lt. de Clermont's car driving away we all stood up. In scrambling out of
the booth we upset a bottle on the table. The fallen bottle tipped
over the ash tray and spilled the ashes and the crumpled cellophane
and finally came to rest against one of the glasses. We all saw it
but none of us stopped to pick it up. It lay against the glass spurt-
ing beer over the table, and the beer ran down onto the bench just
about at the spot where the dark magnolia lay lost in the shadows.

"You owe me two eighty," the bartender said. I threw three
ones on the bar and rushed after the others. As I closed the door I
saw briefly the dripping bottle and all the littered tables, the one
straight chair in front of the bar, the truck driver bent over the
newspaper, and the bartender standing at the cash register. I heard
only the harsh ringing of the cash register.

The warm night and the many stars and the heavy scent of magnolia from a hidden tree wrenched us as if from a deep sleep. "Why didn't you do something?" Ruth said. I wanted to beat her.

"Lt. de Clermont—" Andre began weakly. I was glad for the dark. Our friendship could never have survived the look I gave him. "But you—" he began again hopefully.

"No," I said. "This place. These people. One does not." But I didn't know what it is that one does not.

"I couldn't even faint," Ruth said. I got into the car and slammed the door as hard as I could.

"But to think that Lt. de Clermont," Andre said. Incompleteness was beginning to be our grammar. "A man who did. Who has. Who is."

I hadn't started the car yet, but as we all looked far down the straight-away we could see the red light of Lt. de Clermont's car. As we watched, the light flicked off and we were really in the dark. "Yet," Andre said, "when Lt. de Clermont was ready." Suddenly he laughed. Then I began to laugh and at once the tears ran down my face. I couldn't stop or catch my breath in the agony of my laughter. Ruth and I clung to each other. "Yes," Andre said, "yes." He laughed again and I laughed until I could hear only my own laughter and feel only the convulsive jerks of Ruth's body in my arms.

The Fugitive

"My wife doesn't understand me," George Fuller said. He was surprised to hear himself say it, and he laughed nervously—much the way you do when you come out of a faint and hear yourself actually saying, Where am I? "What we need is another beer," he said. He waved broadly at the fat blonde waitress who was hard to tell in a general way from the bloated blonde whore who sat across the table from him. The waitress brought the beer, and George studied the coins spread on his grimy palm and picked out the price with the filthy broken-nailed fingers of his other hand. Perhaps the waitress was a little cleaner than the whore. "Drink up," he said. "Payday doesn't come every day."

"My wife doesn't understand me," he said, which was a lie of the first remove because in fact what he really had to complain of was that his wife understood him all too well. In fact she understood him completely except for one thing, and even that she was aware of although she refused to understand it.

So when he said, "My wife doesn't understand me," that was also a truth of the second remove, because his wife failed completely to understand his need to retain somewhere within himself a dimension, a complexity, an area of mystery, the essential feeling that there was more to him than met the eye. Except for that one thing he was exactly what met his wife's eye and he knew it.

There are more removes to come but they are dependent upon establishing the identity of George Fuller, which is no simple matter. For instance, in the bar at that moment were no less than three men who would have told you George Fuller was a bag sealer at the can factory across the street and that until recently he had been some sort of a bum.

About the first they were right. They worked in the factory and saw him there every day. But that doesn't tell you much your own eyes haven't already told you. What would be helpful is what you can't be expected to see for yourself, and here the men were quite wrong.

The truth of the matter is that George Fuller was a professor of American Literature, and we will all do well to remember that fact although George himself was trying to forget it. And, lest the academic community take offense, it would be well to add, as

George often told himself, that that was in another city and besides school was out. Is the picture clearer now? No? Let's try it another way.

Year after year George had watched the students go off in the winter to their experience-participation jobs—it was that kind of school—and he imagined them forgetting themselves as students and living into the role of factory worker, office help, nurse's aid, or whatever. It was even rumored that some of the sociology majors worked in a metropolitan whore house, but there was never any evidence that George felt he could admit as valid.

Year after year the students came back and became students again, but they had been somewhere that their reports didn't begin to explain. He could feel it as a barrier between them, and he sensed a subtle change in their relationships, to his own disadvantage.

So it came about that on his way home from the M.L.A. convention in Chicago—incidentally, if it helps any, the title of the paper he gave was "The Dream of the Frontier and the Immaturity of the American Writer" and there were some nuns in the back of the room taking notes—on the way home from Chicago, he got off the train in a good-sized and distant city and found himself a job in a factory making tin cans. His overcoat was long out of fashion, and his baggy tweeds to the eye of the employment manager suggested an outfit got up by the Salvation Army to help a down-and-outer get a new start, but after all it was Christmas time and the employment manager was willing to take a chance.

No, it still isn't going quite right. How about this?

The fall before this—along about October it was—when George told his wife that he planned to be out of town during the work period, she assumed he would be doing research for his book. "What library will you be using?" she said. He hesitated because it hadn't occurred to him that he could keep the secret even from her. "Widener?" she said.

"Yes," he said, "Widener."

"Wonderful," she said. "I haven't seen Elizabeth since you and he were on that panel at Illinois that spring."

"As long as that?" he said, looking for a way out.

"Of course. Don't you remember they were in Europe last time we got to Cambridge?"

"Of course," he said. "Well," he said, "I must admit that I hadn't planned on your going. I wanted this to be strictly work."

"Nonsense. There'll be plenty of time for work and friends too. You know you work better if you have a chance to relax of an evening." It was true.

"Well," he said, "we always get so involved—"

"All right," she said, "what are you up to?"

After all, it wasn't as if he had planned to deceive her. It really had been her leaping to conclusions that put the idea in his mind. "I want to get a job the way the students do."

"Aha," she said.

"Yes, they seem to feel too damn superior when they come back after their brush with *life*—my italics."

"Honestly, George, you baffle me. You're an intelligent man. Surely you must know that if the students feel superior you don't have to feel inferior. Can't you understand that?"

"Of course I understand it."

"Well, then, what's all this about?"

He sighed at the impossibility of explaining but took up the necessary dialogue, which over the years had mercifully been condensed to its simplest terms: one short speech for each of them.

"I understand it but I don't feel it," he said.

"Feeling," she said.

"Well," she said, "it's probably a good idea for you to get this out of your system. You needn't have tried to deceive me."

"No," he said, "that was foolish."

"Where do you plan to be?"

And he gave her the whole plan. How he had checked with the dean to see where the students would be working. How he had found there would be no one at the steel mill at Upton. She complimented him on his strategy and agreed not to try to communicate with him except in a dire emergency. And it all went just as planned except that when he got off the train he didn't get off at Upton and he didn't go to work in a steel mill.

Once he had made his move he wasn't sure he would ever go back. That's what he wanted time to think about. He was now completely free and could move freely. He could turn his back on the dead end his life had worked into. He could make a new start—new name, new job, new infinite possibilities. Still he would regret giving up his job, his career, his books, his wife—how long would it take another woman to unfold herself to him layer by layer like an onion—no, not an onion but something like chard, constantly growing at the center as the outer parts are taken off, even needing to have those parts taken off in order to live? How long if ever?

Now things seem to go much better, don't they? The hardest part of a story is getting started. It never begins where you think—nor ends either, for that matter.

In the can factory George was a bag sealer at $1.12\frac{1}{2}$ an hour. That meant that when the packers finished filling a bag with empty cans he slapped a sheet of cardboard on top and stuck the edges of the bag to it with paper tape. All of which sounds simple enough—even simple-minded—but it involved such things as not getting the tape too wet or too dry and not getting it stuck to itself or to himself because he had to tear it off in long streamers with two long sweeps of his arm to have enough to go around the bags, which were two feet or so square. And it involved getting his fingers stuck together and cutting his hands with the tape. It had looked so easy when the foreman showed him how.

At first the noise of the place cowed him. He huddled under it and concentrated on his work. He was aware, however, of the two packers on the other side of the bins, their eyes focused on the cans coming off the line, their faces intent, almost rapt, darting toward him as they leaned forward to snatch cardboard to put between layers of cans. These packers that he worked with and first saw as devotees, he imagined, even after he knew better, to be praying as they packed, stacked cans like beads that he like a recording angel bundled up to be stored to their piece-work account in the warehouse.

He discovered the first time the line went down that they were not praying, for in the sudden silence he heard the muttered words of a song he vaguely remembered having heard on juke boxes at the campus coffee spots. This was from the young one—younger, that is, thirty-five maybe, thin-faced, dark, wearing a revolting pink sweater in which tiny breasts were all piled up in pathetic points. But you could at least think about going to bed with her, and George Fuller thought about it while he went on sealing the bags left to catch up, fitting new rolls of paper tape into the dispensers, getting a can of water, bringing up new stacks of cardboard and paper bags.

The other packer, the ancient one, might still be praying, he thought at first, for her mouth went on in the silence although it wasn't actually as if she were praying, more like what he imagined chewing snuff would look like. That one was very old. Her hair was white but tinged with yellow like an old man's tobacco-stained beard. It was held tight by a net and looked artificial except that no one would pick out a wig that looked like that. Behind her steel-rimmed glasses her eyes twinkled—shrewdly? maliciously? idiotically? Her face and scalp were pink as if she had just committed suicide by gas.

When the line started up again at rather less than half speed, just a few cans tinkling along now and then, the old woman sprang up and went to work impatiently. The other still sat with her head back against the wall. George jumped to his place and waited tensely, his eye casting around for something to be doing because he saw the foreman coming. He decided to go get water although he had just got a canful. It was useless, however, for the foreman was still there when he got back.

"How do you like it?" the foreman said.

"Fine," George said.

The foreman looked at the seal on a couple of bags. "You're doing fine for a beginner." George felt a glow of satisfaction. That for those students and their superiority.

"OK, Millie," the foreman said, "you work here too."

"F—— you," Millie said without opening her eyes.

George Fuller, who had very rarely heard that word (although it was a commonplace in his reading) and never in the mouth of a woman, dropped a bag of cans. The foreman sprang to his assistance, tucking in the cans that had spilled, replacing bent cans with good ones, and finally repairing the bag with tape. Fortunately the line had just about stopped so no time was lost.

"OK, Millie," the foreman said. "Let's get to work." There was really no work to do. The old woman would stand waiting for the cans to come along in dribbles and then in a lightning-fast motion would scoop up a row of cans with her short-handled wooden fork and fit them snugly into the bag which lay fitted into a metal bin tipped over toward her. Each time, she made the motion as if the belt were delivering at about 120 per cent of capacity. Then she waited. At last, tired of waiting and probably tired of seeing George with nothing to do, she lifted two rows of cans from Millie's partly filled bag and tipped the bin over toward George. Then she sat down.

"OK, Millie, you heard me," the foreman said. The cans were beginning to back up in the line.

Millie at last stood up and in thirty seconds cleared the line. She put down her fork and walked out from behind the bins. George was surprised to see how short she was. "What kind of work did you have in mind for me?" She stopped in front of the foreman. "What kind of work, eh?" She bumped suddenly and then began to grind. Her hips were big enough for a woman twice her size. "What kind of work you got for me?" She held out her arms toward the foreman and shook her shoulders as if she had breasts. God, she was ugly, but George Fuller had to walk around behind a waist-high pile of bags to dissemble his interest.

"I got the work for you all right," the foreman said. He put his hands on her hips. "We'll drink some beer tonight and line up the work until it comes out your teeth." He dropped his hands. "That's tonight. Right now The Can got some work for you—if you don't mind."

A telephone rang nearby. The foreman took it out from behind a post, returned it, and said, "OK, this line's down for the night. Everybody over on seven. They'll start it up right away." He ran down an alley through the towering stacks of bagged cans. The old woman trotted after him.

"Come on," Millie said to George. "I'll show you where to go." She took his arm and led him off through the clanging wilderness. "Thank you," he said.

"You see what it's like," she said suddenly. "What's a single girl to do? She wants some fun. But they only think of one thing. But she has to be careful, living at home, and thinking about getting married some time, and she knows what they're like about their wives when they marry them, untouched. But it's fun, fun, fun for them all the time, and who are they supposed to have fun with I want to know if a girl has to stay untouched for them? And what would he give do you suppose with a wife and five kids? A pat on the ass and a sock on the ear, that's what he'd give, the bastard. They're all alike or all I've ever seen: fun, fun, fun time out of mind, and just because you want a little fun yourself always getting the wrong idea, isn't it?"

"I suppose it is," George said, disengaging his arm and slipping into his jacket.

They walked in silence until they were nearly up to where the old woman was waiting, fork in hand, for the new line to open up. "You know what I mean?" Millie said suddenly, taking his arm again.

"I think I do," George said.

"I thought you would," she said. She walked past the foreman like a burlesque whore, and that was the last time she ever spoke to George.

But it was enough.

That afternoon when he punched out he found a note clipped to his time card: "Millie is a harlotte. Beware. A Friend."

It's hard to explain why George was so terrified by this note written on the back of the wrapper from a candy bar. You, the reader, at once remind yourself that George in any case had only a few weeks to work at The Can. Or any time he wanted he could walk out, go home, work on his book, draw his college pay, which, of course, went on during the students' work period.

You can remind yourself that the scene with Millie ended irrevocably: "That was the last time she ever spoke to George." It seemed at the time like a good resounding way to finish off the scene, to suggest the finality of this for her, to turn the reader back into the story for meditation at that point rather than hurry him forward. It seemed like a fine idea then, but after all maybe it wasn't such a good idea for the story as a whole. Well, it's done now and some element of suspense has been lost for you—but not for George.

George expected at every moment that the conversation would be renewed, but he couldn't run away, not that he had forgotten his book, his college pay, and all the things that you have remembered. But he was beginning to see the dim outlines of a life which might have been his (which might even yet) and of which the germ lay within him, schizoid and terrible—fascinating.

So he was terrified but unable to go away. He was so terrified that he went a long way—how far I can't say—toward becoming what he might under other circumstances have been—that is, a bag sealer and nothing more, incapable forever of the disciplines of detachment and analysis.

The message clipped to his time card ought to have amused him. He should have tossed it away or, better, taken up the game as a way of passing time. He might have analyzed the handwriting, speculated on the strangely biblical *harlotte,* and considered the patterns of literary analogues. But, as I say, he was terrified and resolved to have as little as possible to do with Millie.

The next morning he found a piece of cheap lined paper clipped to his card. There could be no mistaking the hand, large and sprawling as if traced with great care. He was congratulated on having escaped a "whorable fate." The writer (now signed Your Friend) was delighted to have been of use, to find good advice so readily accepted, to have confirmed the belief that he (George) was on the side of good.

For a moment George was ready to believe the whole thing was a hoax: that *whorable* was really too good to be true. But then he was sure there was no one in the plant capable of inventing such a detail. It was difficult for him to believe there was even anyone who could have a subconscious capable of the standard tricks.

On the face of it, however, there were few people who were sufficiently aware of him to write the notes, consciously or not. He considered them through the morning, watched them for signs or absence of signs.

The foreman? Motive: jealousy. Unlikely. He would have been more direct. The old woman? A possibility but she seemed too absorbed in her work even to notice what went on around her. The girl truck driver, who whipped the little fork truck around the warehouse and stacked the cans roof high with furious haste to get back to the *True Love Story* magazine folded open on the seat beside her? He watched particularly when she left her truck and relieved Millie and the old woman for their breaks, but she was too sullen to reveal anything, her eyes downcast at her work. A possibility though. Millie herself? Impossible. Or was it? And there was no one else except himself. He could be mad. A possibility.

By lunch time he had seen nothing suspicious unless it was that he himself, in shredding the wrapper of his mid-morning candy bar, had protested too much. A distinct possibility.

After eating his lunch he left the men's locker room early in order to check his time card, but there was no note. He thought then he would do well to go back to his station and lie down on a pile of empty bags and close his eyes until the line started up. But as he approached the place he saw the old woman sitting on the very pile of bags he had in mind. Her back was toward him. The ends of her hair had been turned under in a roll and held suspended by a net so that it hung free from her head all around like the cap of a toadstool. He could see her cheeks moving like a rabbit's. He was about to duck into an alley to find another place to rest, perhaps at a line that wasn't running that day, when she turned and saw him.

"Howdy," she said. She really said *howdy*. It was the first word he had heard her speak.

"Howdy," he said tentatively as if replying *bon jour* to *bon jour*.

"How you making it?" she said.

"Pretty fair," he said.

"You're doing fine," she said. "Not like those kids or winos."

"Thank you."

"They said you were a wino, but I said no."

He was clearly supposed to say something but he didn't know what it could be.

"No, I told them, not a wino even if he has seen better days— it can't be hid."

"Oh."

"Not for a minute. We could tell the minute we saw you, but they thought it was you were a wino but I said no."

"How can you tell?"

"You just tell. It's not a special thing wrong but you just tell."

That, he guessed, was that—pure mystique. He had no appropriate small talk. However, the back-to-work gong saved him. The old woman sprang to her feet. A stray can rattled at the end of the overhead line but lacked the pressure of other cans to come on down. George and the old woman both looked at it, he still sitting and she in her place with her fork in her hand. Millie and the foreman sauntered toward them. It would be six minutes before cans would begin to arrive at this end of the line.

The message that night read: "Your right. We must part. You explained it so clearly and patiently. It would break his heart if I went with you. We must be strong. Can you ever forgive me? Yours."

George saw at once a new possibility. It could be a simple mistake, the notes getting attached to the wrong card. The fact that there had been no such conversation pointed in that direction —unless it proved he really was mad. He didn't sleep well that night.

However both his hope (that it was a mistake) and his fear (that he was mad) were short-lived, for there was still another note on his card in the morning. His hands shook as he opened it. His eyes jumped all over the paper trying to record it all at once. His brain refused to receive even the shattered words that his eyes did pick up. He could feel his brain grinding in his head like an overloaded machine. He put the note in his pocket and snatched it out again at once but didn't open it. All the while he was briskly walking with the others into the shop. He burrowed into his job.

Throughout the day he studied the note. It got stuck together with glue from his fingers, torn slightly in spite of his care in unsticking it, torn almost in two frantically. It was on the point of disintegration. He knew it by heart, but he had to look at the actual writing to be sure it was real. And each time he looked at it, it said:

> My own— No, we can never part now. I'm so glad you agree.
> You are so wise. You are so thoughtful about your wife that I
> know we will be happy together, but remember she is young
> and can easily get another husband. Now will be a good time
> because we have both our checks.
>
> Your wife
Mrs. George Fuller
>
> P.S. I practise writing it all the time now that we have decided.
> Mrs. George Fuller

And after he put it away, he thought each time that perhaps it really said something quite different, so he took it out again as soon as he could take a minute from his bag sealing. By the end of the day he had covered the entire back of the paper with tape to try to keep it together.

It was clear that he also needed something to hold himself together, and he planned to go as soon as possible to the Workingman's Palace just across the street from The Can.

That night the lines at the checkout were long and slow-moving: it was payday, George's first payday although he had forgotten it. In order to pass the time he began playing himself quick games of tick-tack-toe in the dust on the piles of stock along the pay line.

Others had had the same idea. There were the usual obscenities, insults, invitations written in the dust. And then he saw his name endlessly repeated in the unmistakable writing of the notes: Geor geFullerMrsGeorgeFullerMrandMrsGeorgeFullerGeorgeFuller. The writing would break in the middle of a word and pick up again on the next pile of stock as if it had once been continuous but had been broken by neat earthquakes.

He peered ahead to see if he could catch someone writing, but there was no one. He ran to the head of the line where the writing ended with George Fu, promising to take up again llerMrGeorge on the other side of some unimaginable chasm. He was sworn at and pushed back toward his place, where he was readmitted only with reluctance.

Out on the street half the people in the world were milling around waiting for buses and car pools. The other half were streaming into the Workingman's Palace where a large neon sign in the window now blinked in red and green Payroll Checks Cashed—the S's, of course, crossed vertically by two parallel lines.

Millie and the foreman were getting into a cab, so apparently she, at least, wasn't planning to go off with George that day. The girl truck driver, still reading her *True Love Story,* was filing into a bus. And on the fringes of the crowd trying to get into the bus was the old woman. She was trying to work her way in but didn't have the weight for it.

George was about to cross the street when the old woman saw him. Without leaving her place—although she really had no place to leave—she said, "Going across the street?"

"I thought I would," he said. He was somewhat relieved now although no less in need of a drink.

"Burning a hole in your pocket?" she said. She pulled a long thread of gum from her mouth—so it was gum after all, not snuff.

"It's been a long time," he said, remembering at the last minute his role of Salvation Army bum.

"This'll be the real test," she said and nodded toward the Workingman's Palace.

He was about to recite some pious wish when he became aware of the fact that she was slowly lowering the thread of gum onto her lunch pail in a kind of filigree pattern. She didn't seem to be watching what she was doing, but he was aghast to discover the slow appearance of the unmistakable MrsGeo. Then she was at the bus door, and taking one end of the thread in her mouth she slowly drew it in like spaghetti.

The next thing George knew he was sitting in a booth at the Palace—or at least he assumed it was the Palace, and the flashing sign in the window didn't deny it although he couldn't read it backwards and had to read it in the mirror behind the bar. He was sitting there with a whore. How, you may ask, did he know she was a whore, not, say, simply a B-girl or a lonely girl? Well, since he had been to her room and paid her money, it seemed like a natural enough assumption.

"My wife doesn't understand me," George said, which returns us to the original statement, truth and lie, a lie of the third remove because he was uttering a speech for a role in which he was at the moment luxuriating, and a truth of the fourth remove because, although he was playing a role, it was a role compulsively chosen to give him an opportunity to say exactly that.

"It can't be as bad as that," she said.

"Worse," he said, "much worse. But before we attempt to analyze the ambiguities of the essentially archetypal *bellum sexualis* to which one is committed *ab ovo,* as it were, a war in which defeat for all concerned is probable but in which neutrality is suicide—" He stopped because he saw that she wasn't paying any attention— a good thing too he decided after his first irritation.

She was busy inspecting the men at the bar, smiling at any who looked her way, speaking to several by name.

"What we need is another beer," he said.

"Suits me," she said, the only sign she had heard him. Even then she didn't turn toward him. "How's every little thing, Tom?" she said to a man walking past on his way to the men's room. He was a very hairy man. A thick mane stood up on the back of his neck. Rivers of hair flowed down his arms and spread into deltas at his fingers. A tuft of hair sprang from the open neck of his shirt, and when he bent his head to speak to her he buried his chin in this hair and seemed to have a goat beard tucked into his shirt.

"Just fine," he said. "You going to be around?"

"All night, honey," she said, "for you."

"Save me something nice," he said over his shoulder.

There was a lull then. She had no immediate prospects and turned toward George. "Business is business," she said. And taking up the glass from which she had been drinking all the while,

"Thanks," she said. "Here's looking at you." He raised his glass an inch or two off the table in reply. "I tell you what," she said. "You put another ten with what you gave me and we'll find some nice place to go for the rest of the night, how about it? You can tell me all about your wife" (which shows she had heard him after all), "and I'll write this down in my diary as the night I didn't get hit in the teeth."

"Well," George said. He was considering where spending another ten dollars would leave him for the next week. He completely forgot his traveler's checks and his checkbook deposited in the safe at the Y.

"I've heard of a nice hotel back of the station."

"Why not your place?" he said to get time to think.

"I heard that," a man shouted, and up from the next booth popped the hairy man. "Try to break our date, will you?" And he slapped her so hard that her head bounced off the high back of the booth.

"Just a minute here," George said, struggling to his feet and trying to deploy his chivalry. He had one hand stretched out toward her and the other toward the hairy man. He was very cramped and confused. People kept running up and then running away again without explanation. The back of his head hurt. A rearing horse nearly trampled him. It was *very* important but he couldn't remember it. People were walking all over him.

The light wasn't very good but he could see cigarette butts and he could smell beer and feel it wet under his cheek. He turned his head to avoid the wet and to relieve the pain at the back of his head. The world spun sharply but he steadied himself by the constellations of gum under the table top.

There *were* feet on him. Two extra-large work shoes with bulging safety toes, these with denim legs. Two patent leather pumps, these with silk stockings rolled below the knees and two enormous milk white thighs with blue knots of exploded veins and one large hairy hand. He wasn't sure what the proprieties called for, so he pretended to be asleep.

He hadn't long to wait, however, for the feet were taken off him and the woman said, "What a girl really likes is to have men fight for her."

And the man said, "Yeah."

And the woman said, "I mean it makes you feel romantic and everything."

And the man said, "Yeah."

"Like a princess."

"Yeah."

"Like a dream."

"Get the hell moving up to your place before I have to clout you one," the man said.

"That's what gets me about you, Tom," the woman said.

When they were gone, George Fuller came out from under the table and drank half a dozen whiskeys at the bar. Then he went out to take a bus. It was snowing a little.

He stood for a long time in the snow waiting for the bus, and when it came he was glad of a chance to sit down and get warm. The bus went very slowly, waiting to make its run at a grade when no cars were slewed across the way, spinning its wheels to start, and sliding into the curb whenever it had to stop. He dozed.

When he woke up, the bus was standing still at an intersection in a residential neighborhood. No one was getting on or off the bus. He looked out to see why they were waiting. A girl stepped up onto the sidewalk, having just crossed in front of the bus. She was very close to where he sat and then began to go off in the snow. She was tall, a tall woman even, but her legs had yet no shape to them. She was bareheaded and wore no rubbers or overshoes, just loafers and socks. She was scuffing through the snow. Then she turned her head a little as if she had heard something, perhaps the bus, perhaps to see if someone she knew had come home. But still she didn't turn that far around, not far enough to really see. But he saw her face: the snow melting on her half-closed eyes and her lips parted to receive the small wafers of snow. And he thought, I am dead.

He lay low for a while in his room, didn't go back to The Can or The Palace, and about three days later went to work in the steel mill in Upton.

Oh, the poor bastard.

The Ship

The space was too short to begin with. He had been working in the shipyards long enough to be used to working in cramped places. But he didn't like it. He went through the same reactions each time he had to crawl into a space too small for him and all the work he had to do.

The first thing to do was to look at the job. Look at the job and curse. The cursing was slow and resigned, always without heat. It had nothing to do with a refusal to work. Even when he went up on deck before he struck an arc and told the leaderman what he thought of the whole motherloving business, he knew that he would go down again and start to work.

Then he went down into the forepeak. He repeated the curse formula. But even before he was finished cursing, he started to put on his jacket. It was stiff and cold, the way leather gets when it has been wet and dry. His shirt was already wet from the exertion of hauling his cable to the place where he had to work. He snapped the jacket close under his chin and turned up the collar. He snapped his shield onto his skullguard and pulled on his gloves. He put a dozen rods in his pocket. He looped the cable over his shoulder and climbed onto the tablelike, triangular piece that set into the bow of the ship.

He took the cable off his shoulder and passed it over a pipe to lessen the strain on him. As he passed the holder over the pipe, the bare end of it struck an arc. He blinked. He had no faith that the holder could be passed over the pipe without striking an arc; so he blinked before the arc was struck. Even with his eyes shut he saw a blinding flash of red. And when he opened his eyes, he couldn't see for a moment. He put a rod in the holder and prepared to weld.

The space was definitely too short. There lacked six inches of being enough room for him to stand erect. He tried kneeling, but the strain of holding his arms above his head was too great. He tried backing away, but a beam ran across the deck just behind his head. If he tried to get beyond the beam and low enough so that he could see, he couldn't reach. He stood with the beam against the back of his head. He spread his legs and bent his knees. He humped his back. He twisted his head to the side and back. He started the job.

The paint made it hard. The thick coat of paint over everything made his weld pop and boil as the burning paint bubbled down to the surface of the puddle of weld metal. The puddle broke and dropped down in fiery gobs of molten metal that bathed him in fire. The fire sought out his collar. It found the little hole in his sleeve near the elbow. It seeped in through the unsewed place at the crotch of his right mitten. The paint made it hard. The weld formed slowly, and as it formed it grew to be a series of small bunches rather than a uniform bead. He climbed down from the tablelike piece. He took off his shield and gloves and jacket. He went up to set his machine hotter.

As he came up on deck he felt the chill of the morning air. Where a little rivulet of sweat had run down his back, there was now an icicle. He shivered. The sun was just getting up over Shop Eight, and the disengaged sections of steel booms that had been drifting through the fog began to join themselves into the familiar pattern of ordinary gantry cranes. The layers of fog over the canal began to thin out; where before had been white and black streamers, appeared black water, black swamps and vanishing fog. He knew that as soon as the red sun had finished with the fog, it would turn its attention to heating the deck. He picked his way over the deliriously cablestrewn deck to his machine. The machine was wet with dew. He stood on a snarl of cable to insulate him from the deck while he turned the wet machine ten hotter.

The machine was still too cold. The bead still formed slowly and great drops of metal fell exploding on the deck. He cursed in his shield and stopped welding. He scraped the flux off the weld. A rough uneven weld to be sure, but a weld. For the time being that would do. When he went up for a blow he could set his machine again. But now his legs were tired from the other trip, and he thought only of getting through the day and going home for some sleep.

His arms tired frequently in his cramped position, and he had to stop to rest. Just lowering his arms and raising them was enough rest at first, but after a while he had to stop for a few seconds each time he lowered his arms. Then it was nearly a minute each time, and the rests got closer and closer to each other. Then he had to stop to smoke a cigarette.

After the cigarette he was strong again. Not as strong as at first and he tired sooner. His neck started to get stiff, and the smoke began to make his eyes water. Now he had something else to stop for: he had to wait until his eyes cleared and the smoke dispersed. At first there were long periods between the times when his eyes blurred out, when the tears rolled in rivulets from his eyes and joined with the sweat springing from each pore of his face and the stream running from his nose to form a river rushing over the precipice of his chin and flooding the breast of his leather jacket. When his eyes blurred out, he had to steady himself against the hull and squat on his heels below the level of the smoke until he could see again. Each time as soon as he could see he went back to work. Each time he could stand the smoke and the heat for a shorter period. His jacket became heavy and soggy. His dungarees clung to his legs. His skullguard slipped on his head as the sweatband became slippery with sweat.

He had almost finished the easy side of the first header, and he promised himself a blow when he did finish. The smoke was getting so thick he could scarcely see. His eyes blurred. His mouth gaped for air. His arms ached. They were so tired they gradually dropped away from the weld. The arc popped and sputtered. A great drop fell out of the puddle. It fell inside his collar. He cursed as it rolled down over his tender belly and caught for a second at his belt. He howled as it dragged its fire across his soft groin and shot the length of his leg. He jumped to the deck when it stopped in his shoe. He threw off his shield. He snatched off his gloves. He tore at his shoe, cursing. He knotted the lace. He broke it and tugged at the shoe. He had to stop to loosen the lace. He got the shoe off. And the sock. There was a shallow crater on the top of his foot the size of a dime. It was pink and glistening. He put the shoe on carefully. He did not lace it.

The foreman and the leaderman came down the ladder. The foreman looked at him sitting there and said nothing. He climbed up to look at the weld. "Your machine is too cold," he said. The foreman and the leaderman went through an access hole into number one hold. He sat there and looked after them. His foot ached. He felt a frustrate rage. He wanted to leap after them and beat them with his scaling hammer. He wanted to knock them to the deck and cool his burning foot in the blood he would make gush from their heads. He picked up his wet sock and stuffed it into his pocket. He limped slowly to the infirmary. His foot hurt and he cursed as his heavy shoe chafed the new sore.

When he came back from the infirmary, he went down into the forepeak and began to weld again. The tiredness was gone. The air was clear. But the sun had started its work on the hull, and the whole forepeak was hot and stifling. It seemed as if the tiredness and the heat and the smoke had waited for him there in the forepeak and had started again just where they had left off. They had waited in ambush and had killed his new strength in the first onset. His arms ached. His eyes were dim. Sweat, tears, and snot dripped steadily off his chin, flooding the breast of his jacket just as his strength dripped off him and lay in a puddle on the deck about his feet.

He went down and took a small drink at the cooler. He felt very tired. He shivered inside his wet clothes in spite of the heat of the day. He took a salt tablet and another drink. Force of habit took him to the latrine although he knew he had sweat all the water out of his body. He stood there a conventional time and left. He took another salt tablet and another drink. He remembered that two salt tablets always made him sick. He climbed the gangplank. He felt sick. He hung over the rail. Saliva ran in a stream from his mouth. But he didn't vomit.

He went down the ladder into the forepeak through the column of heat that was rising up the ladder. He got dressed again and started to weld. He felt the tiredness climb onto his arm and swing there. Sweat began to run down his back and legs. Smoke crept into his shield. His eyes watered. His mouth gaped for air.

It was just as he was starting the second header that the noise began. The noise hit him on the side of the head and knocked him off balance. The rod jumped and stuck. He cursed.

The chipper was on the outside of the hull. He was chipping just where the welder was working. There was only the steel hull between them. The pneumatically driven chisel beat against the hull with more than the rapidity of a machine gun. And in the forepeak the sound was magnified, echoed and reechoed from wall to wall of the boxlike room.

Gradually the noise of the chipping settled somewhere in the back of his head and lay there dully. There was an ache that ran all around his head just above his ears. It felt as if the top of his head had been screwed on too tight.

The rod stuck. He tugged at it futilely. He opened the jaws of the holder and left the rod sticking. There was a strange humming in his ears, and his head was stuffed with cotton. It was silence. The chipper had stopped. He had been leaning against the sound for so long that the silence threw him off balance. He felt drunk. The chipper started again.

He climbed out of the forepeak. He looked over the rail. The chipper sat on a scaffold, his legs dangling. He was braced against his gun. His safety hat lay beside him. He was young and golden in the morning light as he looked up at the blackfaced welder looking over the rail.

The welder had his drink and smoke on the ground. But this time the tiredness was waiting for him at the bottom of the gangplank. It hopped on his back as he started up. When he reached the top his legs were trembling and he was panting.

On deck the sound of the chipping was crisp and inoffensive, but as he started down the ladder into the forepeak, the sound rolled up at him, palpable and oppressive as the smoke and the heat. His foot began to hurt. He adjusted the bandage, which had slipped off the burn. The sound of the chipping made him sweat. As he put on his jacket, shield and gloves, he cursed. The muscles of his neck tightened. His eyes felt a pressure behind them. He trembled all over. The chipping never stopped.

He sucked in his breath. The air rushed into him and he felt swollen. He couldn't stop breathing in. It was not a regular breath but seemed to be several together without any air escaping from his lungs. He seemed to stop three times, but each time he sucked in more air rather than let any out. His chest was tight, his head hurt, he was afraid he couldn't get his breath again. His whole face ached with the strain of trying to breathe. And his eyes felt as if they would be shot from their sockets. He tore at his jacket. His breath came back to him, and he felt weak and deflated.

He had almost finished the second header. Just another two inches. His arm ached. Even bracing it in his left hand did no good. His left arm was tired too. He felt his arm dropping. He tried to hold it in place. He ached all over with the strain. His feet slipped on the smooth steel. His arm jerked. The rod stuck. It seemed as if the whole ship was dangling from the end of the rod. The rod slipped out of the jaws of the holder. He sobbed and sat down where he was. All around him the noise surged in vicious waves. It beat upon him. It tugged against his tired arms. It perched between his tired shoulders. It entered into his body with the air he sucked into his gaping mouth. He could feel it within him and without him. The sound slid its slow length around his guts. It tightened gradually the way a man will stretch his arms in a yawn. It was so slow. So strong. So long-enduring. The sound within him finally gave a jerk that squeezed him dry. He got up and went up the ladder.

He was trembling as he came on deck. The sweat was furrowing down his face. It ran in sheets down his back and legs. He could feel water oozing in his shoes as he walked. He took the chipper's hose in his hand, bent it, and squeezed. The noise stopped. He heard the dying hiss of the shutoff hose as the chipper tried his air pressure. He heard the chipper cursing. He saw the chipper's face come over the rail just in front of him. He reached out a hand and pushed the chipper's face. It disappeared. He stepped to the rail just in time to see the chipper's hands slip from the edge of the A-frame that supported the scaffold. The chipper fell against the anchor. His head hit solidly. It reminded the welder of the time he stole a coconut from the A&P on the way home from school. He held it in his hand and smashed it against the curb, and the warm milk splashed over his hand. The chipper dropped into the water.

A needle fish darted away just before he hit. The welder turned and went down into the quiet of the forepeak.

The men stormed down the gangplank at 3:25 and carried with them the few of the second shift that the warning whistle had caught on the way up. They hurried to put away their tools and get ready to get out of the yard. By 3:30 they were hanging back away from the clockhouse near the lockerroom and the warehouse. When the whistle blew there was a rush. The safety inspectors shouted and threatened, but the rush had already piled up long lines of men waiting to punch out and get their checks. There was talking and laughter between the lines as one filed rapidly ahead or another was held up. There was talk of beer, and there were bets on who would be the first to make it to the place where they cashed their checks. And when they had passed through the clockhouse, they compared the numbers on their checks to see who would win the pool. They waited to pick up their rides, and then they strode intently off among the cars, Indian file, in small parties.

The first shift swaggered into the bar with the air of men beating their way through swinging doors. At the farther end of the bar, which ran along two sides of the room, a small group milled about brandishing their checks. A girl behind the bar passed a fountain pen from one to the other and vanished into the back room with the signed checks. She returned with her hands full of money and threw it on the bar in front of the proper men. They took their money and stood up to the bar and ordered their drinks, always needing one more to settle the score.

The welder stood among the men waiting to cash their checks. The verticals of perspiration tracks in the grime of his face accentuated his gauntness. His hard hat was pushed back on his head. A man he knew vaguely as Slim from McComb bought him a beer. "This the third week in a row I bought the beers," Slim from McComb said. "I hope next week someone else has low in the check numbers."

"Thanks," the welder said. He took a long drink from the bottle. It was cold and bitter and tasted good.

"Going to cash your check?" Slim from McComb said.

"I guess so," the welder said. He took the pen that the girl held out to him. He put the check on the bar, picked it up, and turned it over and stared at it. The girl twisted her neck around so she could see the check. "Be sure to sign it Mike Collins," she said.

He wrote it slowly. It was difficult to write. It looked strange when it was finished. He passed the check over the bar and waited. He up-ended the beer bottle, emptied it, and set it down on the bar with a bang. The girl slapped a handful of bills on the bar in front of him. "Sixty-five dollars," she said. He picked it up and stuffed it into his pocket. Turning toward the other end of the bar, he ordered two Regals and asked for a dollar's worth of nickels.

He took the beer and the nickels over to where Slim from McComb was furiously shaking hands with a onearmed bandit. "Here's a beer," he said. "I hope it's as good as the one you gave me."

"Sure thank you," Slim from McComb said. "You want to get here? This my last nickel." He dropped the nickel into the slot and pulled the lever slowly. The wheels spun in wobbling streaks of variegated color and jerked to stops one after the other. "I guess I'll buy beer with my nickels from now on," Slim from McComb said.

Mike stepped up to the machine with his hand full of nickels. He set the beer on top of the machine and began throwing nickels into the slot. He jerked the lever and the wheels spun madly, and he sipped his beer, watching the wavering streaks of color through halfclosed eyes. The wheels jerked to stops and he lost. He lost and won. Lost more than won, but got back a little now and then. The talking and the laughter, the driving jive of the juke box became louder and more confused, blending into an amorphous roar that from time to time beat into his consciousness. He tried to brush it aside with his hand, but it beat insistently on his head. The sound, pure noise, beat on and on. It would not go away. It made him sweat.

Then Slim from McComb said, "Have another on me."

"OK." Slim from McComb left to go to the bar. Mike became intent on the slot machine and slugged down the beer before Slim came back with more. The noise was gone.

Slim from McComb brought him the coldbeaded bottle just as he finished the other. Mike sipped it. "Just as good as the other," he said. He dropped a nickel into the slot and yanked the lever.

"It's all good," Slim from McComb said. "And speaking of stuff that's all good, I got to be taking off. I got a date with the only girl I ever met who was hot in the pants as I am." He set his halfempty bottle on top of the machine and left. The noise of the bar swirled after him and surged back upon Mike, pulsing within and all around him. The wheels of the machine jolted to successive stops. He heard the rain of slugs in the cup. He turned back to the machine. He had hit the jackpot.

Mike's hands trembled as he scooped up a double handful of the slugs. He spilled a few on the floor and laughed hysterically. The men around the machine scrambled to pick them up. "Keep them. Keep them," Mike said. His voice was shrill. "Buy beers." He set the slugs back into the cup and picked up the jackpot coin. He held it flat in his hand and stared at it.

"That's worth ten dollars," a man said.

"I guess I'll keep it for good luck," Mike said. He picked up his dripping bottle and went out into the street, thinking of Slim from McComb and of a little place down the street he had heard about.

The sidewalk had the pleasant roll of a ship at sea. Mike staggered slightly and blinked his eyes at the light. He was surprised that it was not night. The beer and the bar and the noise had prepared him for night. It was incredible that it should still be afternoon. It seemed as if there should be the quiet softness of forsaken night. But the afternoon was harsh, and the beer bottle he held in his hand became a little foolish.

The next bar Mike went into—he was sure it was the place he had heard about—was smaller than the first place, dingier and darker. He slammed the empty bottle on the bar. "How will you trade me?" he said.

The fat man on the high stool behind the bar chewed his cigar over to the side of his mouth and kept polishing beer glasses. "The empty bottle and fifteen cents to boot," he said. "I'll open the new one free."

"It's a deal. And throw in a couple more for my friends." Mike indicated by a wave two men at the other end of the bar.

"OK. But it will cost you fifteen cents apiece to have them opened." The fat man quivered a bit on the high stool and slid ponderously to the floor. The two men at the other end of the bar raised their glasses to Mike and went back to their conversation.

Mike looked around the place. There was a latticework partition separating the bar from a dusky room beyond. There were tables in the room and a cleared space for dancing. Off in a far corner was the red glowering of a juke box, but now it was silent.

A shadowy woman sat at a table against the lattice. She rested her head in her hands. And her long hair fell forward over her hands. She was motionless.

"She drunk or asleep?" Mike said.

"She feels sad," the fat bartender said.

"Why is she sad?" Mike said.

"She just gets sad sometimes," the fat bartender said.

Mike walked over to her table. "Hello," he said. "Want a beer?" If the girl heard he couldn't tell. She remained motionless. He reached out his hand to touch her. He stopped. He touched her. She didn't respond. She neither shook off his hand nor rose under it. "Want a beer?" he said again. "Make you feel better." She remained motionless. He dropped his hand.

He backed slowly away from her table and sat down at the table on the other side of the door facing her. He leaned his forehead toward hers and propped his head in his hands. His skull-guard slid forward over his eyes. Even so the thought of the girl oppressed him. Her face that he had never seen was like the face in a dream, shifting incessantly, never clear. Dark or fair. Sullen. Crushed and hopeless. Proudly rebellious, shouting against fate. And what was the fate that had bowed her head and strewn her hair in sorrow over her hands? His continued brooding over the girl made him melancholy. The dim light of evening faded slowly through him. It was a quiet time, serene, a time of relaxation or resignation. He drifted into a sort of twilight stupor.

When he lifted his head again, the faint twilight had given way to hard electric light. He stepped to the door of the bar and stood hanging on to the frame for a moment. The room was bright and filled with smoke. Men were massed along the bar like thunder-clouds along an August horizon. A man stepped from the street into the doorway at the other end of the bar. He stood for a moment blocking the door. A tall heavy middle-aged woman staggered along the bar and beat the newcomer on the shoulder. "Heavy, you old muffadite, how you been?" she shouted in his ear.

"Fine, May, you old whore, just fine." He put his arm around her and gave her bottom an experimental slap. She giggled.

"Let's have a beer," she said. They went off down the bar.

Mike edged close to the bar to order a beer for himself. He took the bottle in his hand and began to wander along the bar. Suddenly remembering the girl with the sorrowful hair, he turned and ran to the table where she had been. She was gone. He spat a mouthful of beer into the chair where she had been sitting. He staggered across the dance floor, finishing the bottle as he went. He had almost reached the word MEN painted crookedly on the door of a boarded-off corner when he saw a girl sitting with her hair over her hands. He stepped toward her. But she lifted her head and

laughed, and he knew she was not the girl. She turned and saw
him staring, and her eyes were suddenly hard but her mouth went
on laughing as she slowly turned back to the man opposite her. The
man looked up at him and they both laughed. Mike stood there
unwilling and unable to break away, rocking with indecision. He
pulled a crumpled bill from his pocket and threw it on the table
between them. And making a gesture which he conceived to indicate graphically what their impotence could do with the money,
both his and hers, yes, the rest of the laughers, he set the empty
bottle beside the door as one going to bed sets out a milk bottle. He
opened the door and went into the men's room.

The stench of the place gagged him. He stepped carefully,
trying not to touch anything. The fixtures were filthy and the floor
was awash. He tried to walk without touching the floor. He lost
his balance and fell against the wall. As he straightened he saw
a small sticker advertising prophylactics: Don't Take A Chance.
Another sticker giving the location of the nearest army greenlight
station. A small machine for dispensing safes. Intrigued, he
dropped a quarter in the slot and turned the handle. Furtively he
put the box in his pocket without looking at it.

A lean young man came in and stood beside him. He had an
unlighted cigarette in his mouth. "Got a match?" he said.

Mike looked around vaguely. He picked a book of matches off
the side of the scrimy washbowl. "Here you are. Keep them. Keep
them."

"Cigarette?" the lean young man said. He held out a beat-up
pack.

Mike took one. "Got a match?" he said. The young man passed
over the matches. "Thanks," Mike said.

"You work out at Delta?" the lean young man said buttoning
his fly.

"I'm a welder."

"You're a sucker. What do you make? A hundred a week?"

"Not that much," Mike said.

"Want a drink?" the lean young man said. He pulled a pint from his coat pocket.

"Don't mind if I do," Mike said. He grabbed the bottle and drank deeply.

"Take it easy. Take it easy."

"Plenty more where that came from," Mike said. He fished a handful of bills out of his pocket. "The next pint's on me." Mike killed the pint and threw the bottle to the floor. It crashed loudly on the concrete. He became furious at the sound and stamped out crunching the broken glass under his heavy work shoes.

As he came out of the men's room, he caught a glimpse of the girl with the sorrowful hair passing through the bar and going out into the street. He lurched forward. He was close to being sick. The figures of the men at the bar became indistinct. He could concentrate only on the rectangle of the door to the street. Everything else faded. The door burned into his mind as a necessity of paramount importance. He had to reach it. He walked faster. He started to run. He had to get to the door before the closing mist enveloped him. It settled closer and closer. It swam before his eyes. He shook his head to throw it off. His eyes were almost out. He fell down the steps to the sidewalk.

He ran off the top step and continued to run in the air. He rolled into the street battering his unfeeling body on the pavement. He crawled on his hands and knees to the building and pulled himself up. He had to keep going. He had to find the girl with the sorrowful hair. He put his hand in his pocket and brought it out clenching the package of safes. He felt sickness coming on. It crowded into his throat. It clutched at his stomach.

The wall turned and he followed it into an alley. He stopped for a moment. His knees buckled and he fell on his face. He got to his knees and hung over an overturned barrel. He was violently sick.

His churning stomach and gaping mouth wrenched him back

to consciousness for a moment. Then he sank down a giddy abyss, hoping feverishly for oblivion.

The next time he woke up he was lying on his back. Two men were bending over him, going through his pockets. He tried to get up but they held him down. He struggled. They held him, and he felt a heavy blow on his ribs. He fell back.

Someone said, "You're too handy with that knife."

Someone said, "To hell with it. He's drunk."

The men went through his pockets. He felt himself slipping down and getting further away from them. They faded away and away. For a moment he saw the girl with the sorrowful hair standing behind them. He could almost see her face. He tried to reach toward her, but one of the men held him with one hand and continued to go through his pockets with the other. He tried to reach toward her, but the effort was too great. He succeeded only in twitching the fist that held the safes. He heard one of the men say, "—jackpot coin from a slot machine. Keep it. It's good luck." There was a gigantic pounding in his head. The noises of the shipyard. The sound of pneumatic hammers. It beat inside his head and deafened him. He tried to put his hands to his ears, but the effort sent him spinning down a long pit toward black water.

There was blackness all around him. The water below him showed no reflection of light. The speed of his fall increased. The sound of the hammers grew louder. Just before he hit the water he struggled for a moment. Some last reserve of strength helped him to move his arms and legs and shout weakly. Then the water was close. The black water stood just below him. Even as he hit, even in the darkness, he saw a phosphorescent flash. He knew it was a needlefish darting away.

The Night of the Two Wakes

In all my life up until now I have been to two wakes, and they were both on the same night. From the time I was little, I had heard about wakes: so about two o'clock they put down the lid on the coffin and dealt out a hand of cards, and they knocked on the coffin and said, Will you take a hand of cards? but he didn't say anything; then about four o'clock they asked him again and he didn't say anything, so they took him out and stacked him in the corner and dealt the cards at him and asked him if he wanted a drink and he didn't say anything, so they threw a drink at him; and, oh, but he had a breath on him at the funeral and a deck of cards where his prayerbook should have been. I would never even have seen a corpse except that some howling old woman in black dragged me up to my father's casket when he was laid out under his mounds and mounds of flowers.

This night of the two wakes was a night in one of the summers I worked for old man Baker up near Boston. Baker had a restaurant in a small chain that tried for a while to run in competition with Howard Johnson. The poor bastard was going bankrupt on the place. I think he was losing his mind, and I know damn well he was ruining his health, all the time worrying and trying to get along completely without sleep. But he was an old man and we were college kids, and it was almost impossible for us to feel very much for him.

On this particular night we were planning to go to Red Farrell's wake right after work. Business had been slow all night, so we started about midnight to do the work we usually did after we closed up. We washed the floors and cleaned the grills and put away the food in the big icebox. We even went off upstairs one by one to get our showers. We put on clean shirts and drew to-morrow's fresh white pants from the linen room because none of us kept good clothes at the store.

The store was empty when I went and told old man Baker that it was two o'clock. He was standing beside the front door looking out. He looked at his watch and then out at the yard again, and we both held our breath while a car pulled into the yard, but it only turned around and headed back toward Boston. Old man Baker closed the door and locked it and turned off the sign and nodded good night and went off upstairs to figure the cash although it was a good bet that he'd be asleep with his head on the desk when we got back.

As we went out through the kitchen we took a little of this and a little of that to eat along the way, things we weren't supposed to have: a few almonds, a slice of cold chicken, an orange. Then we were all set to take off for Red Farrell's wake.

Red Farrell was a kid who had worked right along with us in the store. He never was a fast man on the grill, and he couldn't remember more than ten kinds of ice cream. He'd rather sit in the stock room and peel potatoes than work out front, and he'd rather throw half-pint milk bottles at rats than anything. He didn't even know enough to love up the waitresses when they came out to the stock room to grab a quick smoke or to fix their stockings. But everyone liked him, even the girl who was mad at him because she had made every other kid who ever came to work at the store. And then on his day off Red just went under in the middle of the lake without even a yell or anything, and we were going to his wake after work.

As we stood beside the cars for a minute—Billy the Cork, Billy Murph, Bill Johnson, and I together, and Primo the dishwasher alone beside his old Chevvy—Bill Johnson said, "There he is already." We all looked up and saw old man Baker sleeping with his head on the desk up in the office. Bill Johnson, who was a kind of assistant manager and who would have to figure the cash if Baker didn't, threw a handful of pebbles against the screen, and Baker sat up quickly and we could see his lips moving and his pencil going slowly down the long register tape.

We were just going to get into the car when Primo said to me, "Thanks for helping me in the kitchen." When we had our own work pretty well in hand, Johnson had sent me out to help Primo finish up on the dishes.

"That's OK," I said.

"We all help each other here," Johnson said. Primo was the one who came to work after Red died. The old dishwasher moved out front with us to take Red's place, and the new man became the dishwasher. That was our way. We had all come in as dishwashers, and I for one still liked to get out back and take off my shirt and tie and go to work on the old machine.

"I didn't want to be held up tonight," Primo said.

I'm not good at noticing things, but even I could tell he was trying to say something. "How come?" I said.

"My mother's wake," he said.

"You should have stayed out," Johnson said.

"If it wasn't a new job I would," he said.

"We would have covered for you," I said.

"Thanks anyway," Primo said. He started to get into his car. The rest of us looked at each other. Since we had made up our minds to go to a wake anyway, it was an easy matter to make it two. Primo told us to tail him through the tunnel to East Boston.

Billy the Cork had a hard time tailing Primo because Primo just took off and never looked back. Even when he squeaked through a red light that caught us, he didn't slow down, and it was only luck that we caught him at the tunnel. It wasn't too far from there to his house, but there were so many twists and turns down narrow dirty streets that I was beginning to wonder how we'd ever get out again, especially with Billy the Cork all the time driving with one hand and eating raw frankfurts he had brought along in his pocket. Finally we followed around a corner that Primo had taken just as fast as any other, and we were just in time to see him jump out of his car and cross the sidewalk and dive into the doorway of a tenement. Billy the Cork wasn't able to stop until we were half way up the block. Then we got out and started to go back.

"What a wild man," Billy the Cork said.

"You'd think he didn't want us," Bill Johnson said. We all stopped in front of the door. "I don't want to go in if he don't want us," Bill said.

"We come quite a ways," Billy the Cork said.

"If they don't want us we better go back," I said.

"Maybe he just went in to say we were coming," Billy Murph said. "Strangers and all."

"Maybe," I said. So we went up to the door and opened it. There was a long flight of stairs going right up from the door, and there was no one in sight, and there was no sound at all from up-stairs although by the light on the wall up there we could tell the door was open. Then my big feet kicked over a milk bottle. It didn't break but there was a lot of noise.

"It's no good pretending we aren't here now," Johnson said and started up the stairs. The rest of us followed along.

At the top of the stairs we hesitated again. We could see part of a room in which there were no people but only rows of folding chairs arranged as if someone were going to give a speech or show colored slides. Even out in the hall I could smell the suffocating stink of the flowers. "This is the place all right," I said.

"But is it the place for us?" Billy the Cork said. "It's weird." We could hear men crying in another room, saying, Mama, Mama, and one of them every once in a while saying, Papa, you've got to be strong, and both crying and saying, Mama, Mama.

We all looked at each other and Billy the Cork said again, "Is it the place for us?" Nobody paid any attention to him. But a little dog came out and began barking like crazy. Still nobody came out to see what the matter was. Billy the Cork gave the dog the last of his frankfurt, and the dog crawled away under a chair to eat it. We stepped into the room, keeping close together and moving very slowly.

The room wasn't completely empty. There was an old man sleeping in one of the folding chairs in the back of the room. He was turned sideways and rested his head on his arms on the back of the chair. He had a fierce growth of white beard and looked as if he hadn't moved out of the chair for three days. He was wearing a grey coat sweater over a white shirt that was buttoned but had neither collar nor tie. In the front of the room there was a doorway that gave onto a limitless bank of flowers. In the midst of the flowers a candle was burning, and we all veered toward it, walking softly on the threadbare carpet with its faded roses.

This room too seemed at first to be empty except for the masses of flowers—whew—and the casket, but the Mama, Papa, Mama crying was louder here, and then we could see Primo in his dirty white pants kneeling before a small old man who was sitting in a little alcove at the end of the room across from the casket. Billy the Cork and Billy Murph stepped up to the casket and knelt, blessing themselves and glancing into the casket at the same time. Then they bowed their heads and remained motionless.

"What am I supposed to do?" Bill Johnson said in my ear.

"Just go up and take a look," I said. "Kneel on the foot stool. Bow your head and count a hundred slow."

"That all?"

"Keep your eyes open," I said. "That's all I'll be doing." I was trying to avoid looking at Primo and his father, and I was trying not to read the cards on the flowers, and I was trying not to seem to watch the two Billys praying, but they were taking so long about it that I looked back at them. "Better make it a hundred and fifty," I said to Bill. The two Billys blessed themselves together and stood up together. Bill and I stepped forward. I got down all right, but you could tell that Johnson wasn't used to kneeling because his knee hit with a terrible thump. Even in the candle light I could see how red his face was, and I had all I could do to keep from laughing.

The woman in the casket was more or less what I expected Primo's mama to be. She was fat. Her hair was still black. A rosary spilled over her stumpy fingers. Her face was painted so that she looked like a whore, but no amount of paint could hide the heavy mustache and the pockmarks. I bowed my head and began to count slowly.

When we stood up and started back toward the two Billys, Primo left his father and came toward us. He shook hands silently with all of us, starting with Bill Johnson. "Will you speak to my father?" Primo said. We shuffled uncomfortably and Primo turned his back on us and walked toward his father. We followed. "Papa," Primo said, "this is Mr. Johnson from the restaurant and some of the other boys who work there."

The old man sat up straight in his chair and looked sharply at us. "Mr. Johnson?" he said and started to struggle out of the chair.

"Don't get up, please, sir," Bill Johnson said. "We only want to express our sympathy."

"And the sympathy of everyone at the store," Billy Murph said.

"Mr. Baker wants you to know how very sorry he is he couldn't come over with us," Billy the Cork said.

"We never knew her," I said, "but we can tell she was a fine woman."

"Only a fine woman could have brought up such a fine hard-working son as Primo," Bill Johnson said. That was a relief to me because although I knew we had to say she was a fine woman, I couldn't think of anything fine to say about her—the rouged face, the pockmarks, the mustache.

"Only a fine woman would have so many friends to send her such fine flowers," Billy Murph said.

"Only a fine woman would be missed so by her little dog," Billy the Cork said.

The old man began to weep large tears, and he covered his face with his hands. "Oh, Mama, Mama, Mama," he said.

"Papa, Papa, you've got to be strong," Primo said.

"You have a fine son to comfort you," Bill Johnson said.

"That's a blessing," Billy Murph said.

"And you've got the girls to be strong for," Primo said. The old man had stopped crying. Primo suddenly shouted, "Mama, Mama, Mama," and buried his head in his father's lap. The old man bent over him and cried with him.

We all looked at each other and started to leave. "Maybe we should wait to say goodbye to Primo," Billy Murph said. We sat down in the folding chairs in the outer room, but we had hardly settled ourselves when we heard women's shoes banging on the stairs.

"Let's be getting out of here," I said. We broke for the door and reached it just as two girls were about to come in. They stopped and we stopped. They must have been the sisters all right though God knows where they were coming from at that hour. They wore tight black dresses and black shoes and stockings. Their black hair was loose. They had no jewelry or make-up. Their faces were quiet and sad. They were striking women. After the slightest of hesitations they came in and nodded gravely as they passed us, but once they were inside the room they broke into an awkward graceful feminine run. As they entered the other room they turned to run toward their father. It was hard to tell if they looked back at us.

"Perhaps we should still wait," Billy the Cork said.

Then in the other room the girls began hysterically without any buildup, Papa, Papa, and the men began, Mama, Mama.

"Let's get the hell out of here," I said.

"Amen," Bill Johnson said.

We went back to the car and cruised around a bit looking for a bar, but everything was shut tight by then. "At a proper Irish wake we'll get whiskey," Billy the Cork said.

"That's right," Billy Murph said, "and none of that crazy yelling. Don't worry, Bill, there won't be anything like that."

"I'm not worrying," Johnson said.

"If there's one thing the Irish know, it's how to run a wake," Billy the Cork said, and he took us the shortest way to Red Farrell's house.

Red's house wasn't very far from the store. It was on a quiet back street in a suburban town. The houses were all larger than they have been built for a good while now, but each was a one-family house set close to the street with a small lawn and just enough room on either side to back in a coal truck.

Even before we were set to ring the bell, the door was opened for us by a large man perhaps ten years older than any of us. He was dressed in a good dark suit and looked very fresh despite the fact that it was already nearly four o'clock. "We're from the store," Bill Johnson said while the rest of us were trying to get into the right positions and get our faces fixed right.

"I'm Red's brother," the man said. He shook hands with Johnson and gently urged him through the door and turned him left into a parlor. To each of us as we passed he said, "I'm Red's brother," and as we mumbled our names he passed us in and turned us firmly left.

There weren't many flowers but there were enough for a great stink. As Johnson and I walked toward the casket I looked slyly for flowers with our card on them, but I couldn't see any. We knelt together quietly, and as I blessed myself I felt his arm moving beside me. I looked quickly at him and saw him finishing a highly professional sign of the cross. Then I looked at Red.

Red was pale as death and very waxy-looking—there was a suffocating blanket of pinks right under my nose. He didn't look like anybody who would care about throwing bottles at rats or turn his head away while a waitress fixed her stocking. He didn't look good to me at all. I bowed my head and heard Johnson whisper, "Two hundred."

"Three hundred," I whispered, "three hundred for old Red." I started off with an Our Father, counting the words on my fingers as I said them. But51 deliver52 us53 from54 evil55. Amen56. 57 thousand, 58 thousand, 59 thousand, 60 thousand. On the second hundred I tried a Hail Mary just for variety, and that came out to 42. On the third hundred I said them one after the other, and they added up almost exactly right: hour94 of95 our96 death97. Amen98. 99 thousand, one hundred thousand.

I raised my head just a trifle and saw out of the corner of my eye that Johnson was raising his too. He moved his arm beside me and as I felt it move I made the sign of the cross with him. We stood up together and as we stepped away from the casket, Billy the Cork and Billy Murph stepped up like one man. I wanted to take a quick look around for our flowers and keep tabs on how long the two Billys took with their prayers for Red, but the brother took us both by the arm and led us out of the room.

"A tragic thing," Johnson said as we walked through the dining room.

"Really tragic," the brother said. He continued to grip our arms and urge us along. "He had just about decided he had a vocation, you know, and now this. Really tragic."

"Mr. Baker wants you to know how really sorry he is he couldn't come over with us," I said.

"Some girls from the store were over earlier tonight," the brother said. "They were fine girls."

"He was a fine boy," Johnson said.

"Only a fine boy would be missed like that by girls like those," I said.

"How are the parents taking it?" Johnson said.

The brother stopped us at the door to the kitchen. "Hard," he said. "Very hard. He was the baby, you know, and with a vocation too. You boys know how it is for the old people to have a son with a vocation."

"That's hard," I said.

"Through the mercy of God they're sleeping at last," he said.

"The mercy of God," Johnson said.

I nodded gravely and the brother shoved us into the kitchen. "I'll get you a beer," he said and went to the refrigerator.

There were three old men in shirtsleeves sitting at a bare kitchen table, drinking beer and playing twenty-one. Only the one facing the door looked up as we came in. The other two could tell from his face that we weren't worth looking at. "Hit me," one of the men said. The dealer dealt him a card. The man knocked on the table with his knuckles, and the dealer dealt him another card. "I'm good," the old man said.

The dealer turned up his cards and studied them, and he studied the other hands on the table. He salted his beer and dealt himself one card. "I'll pay nineteen," the old man said. He ran his finger inside the neck band of his shirt, which was fastened by a gold stud but had neither collar nor tie.

The brother brought back two cans of beer with little knobs of foam standing up from the punched holes. We took the beer gratefully because it had already been a long night and a lot of death. We lifted our cans toward him and drank. "Wait here," he whispered, "I'll go get the others."

Johnson and I sat down in some chairs against the wall away from the table. The beer was cold. The room was cool—and quiet, too, except for the murmured ritual of the game. The white curtains blew from the window, and the open door rattled softly at its hook. A vine scraped lightly at a shutter. The soft night noises and the freshness of roses filled the room. Even the first few sips of beer made me sleepy.

Johnson got up from his chair and walked over to the table. He reached for the salt and lost his balance, bumping heavily against the table. The old men stood up quickly. Their quick hands grabbed their beer so that none spilled except a little of Johnson's. He reached again for the salt and salted his beer. He came back toward me with the dark wet spots on his shirt and pants. The old men sat down again. They hadn't looked at him. They went back to drinking and watching and knocking.

Only the one facing the door looked up when the two Billys came in. The other two looked at him, and then they all looked back at their cards. The brother went to the refrigerator, and the two Billys sat down in the row of chairs with us. I hadn't been able to keep a very accurate count on them what with interruptions and forgetting which hundred I was working on, but they must have taken close to a thousand, the show-offs.

The brother brought us all beer. We lifted our cans toward him, but he pointed through the dining room. We all turned in our chairs and lifted our cans again. "Red," Billy the Cork said, and we all said, "Red." The brother's jaw was stuck way out, and his eyes were beginning to shine moistly. He turned to the refrigerator to get beer for the card players. He filled their glasses without speaking to them, nor they to him. Even between hands they acted as if he wasn't there. One of the old men picked up his box of matches to light his pipe, but the box was empty. All the old men fumbled in their pants pockets and in the pockets of their sweaters, which hung over the backs of their chairs, while the brother went and got fresh boxes for everyone. The old men all lighted their pipes and went on playing.

"Let's get out of here," Johnson whispered to me.

"We'll have to wait," I said.

Johnson turned to Billy the Cork and whispered, "Let's get the hell out of here."

"The beer is cold," Billy the Cork said.

And Billy Murph leaned over and said, "Where else will you get beer at this hour?"

"I've had it," Johnson said. "I want to get some sleep."

"Stick around," Billy the Cork said.

"See how the Kerrymen drink their beer and stay awake," Billy Murph said.

"How about Galway?" I said. "How about that?"

"Galway?" Billy the Cork said. "So now it's Galway with you. I've heard you say different."

"God damn the counties of Ireland," Johnson said. One of the card players rapped loudly on the table. "Sorry," Johnson said, turning a bright red.

"Yes, now it's Galway," I said. "Tonight in this house for Red it's Galway."

"Out of respect for Red," Billy Murph said.

"Yes, out of respect for Red," Billy the Cork said, "but we don't have to respect you."

"Respect Red, respect Galway, respect me," I said. "All or nothing." The card players weren't watching us, but I was watching them. Our voices had got quite loud, but the card players went on playing slowly and knocking softly.

"Hold on, hold on," the brother said. He was opening beer cans furiously and ran with them to us.

"They want a fight," I said. I drank off half the new can of beer.

"Now look," Billy the Cork said. He bobbed right up in front of me and shoved his face up into my face. "That's not so and you know it, but I'm damned if anyone can make me say that Kerrymen don't want a fight, right, Murph?"

"Right," Billy Murph said.

"See," the brother said, "no one wants a fight. Drink up, boys."

"Kerrymen always want a fight," Billy the Cork said, "right, Murph?"

"Right."

"By God, I want a fight for Galway," I said. We were yelling now.

"Boys, boys," the brother said. "This is a quiet neighborhood."

"Not any more," Johnson said.

"Remember the parents," the brother said.

"Right," Murph whispered.

"I'll fight you," I whispered. "Step out that door."

"The first one that makes a noise is an Englishman," Billy the Cork said.

"Drink up, drink up," the brother said, but we were all out the door by then.

We found ourselves in a grassy back yard overlooked by the windows of at least three houses. I arranged myself against the side of the house, and they stood before me, one a little to either side. I looked at all the dark windows and tightly shut doors. The night was so quiet that I heard one of the players rap on the table. I was about to issue my challenge, but mindful of the restriction of silence I just held out my arms. They came at me cautiously.

None of us made any attempt to strike a blow. It wasn't that kind of a fight. We just came together and grappled. For a long time it was my right arm against Billy Murph and my left arm against Billy the Cork. They turned me from the side of the house and pushed me around pretty much, but it was slow work for them because I was a little bigger than the one and half a foot bigger than the other. We waltzed twice around the yard in slow time. Sometimes my feet were off the ground. I was turning all the time because of the stronger pressure Billy Murph could apply to one side. Then they worked me into the middle of the grass and, as if they had done it many times before, each put a leg behind me and pushed.

The fall knocked the breath out of me, and I just lay still for a while, and they lay on me, their arms locked around my arms and their legs around my legs. And then by God I stood up. Oh, I was a giant. As I came up they were hanging all over me like hounds on a bear, and I shook Billy the Cork off, and I pushed Billy Murph over him, and I piled the one on the other and jumped on top, and I rested.

I had been aware during the last of the fight of sirens fading in from the distance, but it was like crowds shouting and cheering, and it urged me on. Then as I lay on the other two, I heard a car stop in the street. A spot light hit one of the houses in the back. Lights came on in another. I jumped up and Murph was up like a jack-in-the-box. I threw Billy the Cork onto his feet. The whole yard was bright. Men were running in the gravel drive. Someone yelled, "Through here." We just stood.

Johnson was standing on the back steps yelling, "Did you get them? Which way did they go?"

"We had them but they got away," Billy Murph yelled, pointing toward the side of the yard the spot light couldn't hit. As he said it and pointed, a powerful flashlight hit him and he held his pose, all in white pointing off into the night.

"They were all in black," Billy the Cork said. "They'll be hard to find." Two policemen ran past without speaking.

The brother came out and ran half across the yard after the policemen and stopped. The two Billys and I went into the house and took two cans apiece from the refrigerator and an opener from the sink.

"How was it?" the dealer said.

"All Galway," I said. My face hurt when I smiled. My shirt was torn half off. Tomorrow's pants had grass stains at the knees.

"Good boys," the dealer said and dealt the cards.

"Let's get the hell out of here," Johnson said, but by then we were half through the dining room on our way out.

As we were turning into the yard at the store we saw four of the waitresses cutting across the yard to their rooming house. We asked them where the hell they were coming from at that hour, and they told us they had gone swimming after the wake. We gave them each a can of beer, and then we took them up to the bunk room. Old man Baker was sleeping in his car when we went past, and he was still there an hour and a half later when I came down to open the store for the day. After I gave the girls their breakfast—with large orange juice, which the help wasn't supposed to have—and after they had got out of sight, I squeezed another large orange juice and took it out to old man Baker. It seemed the only decent thing to do.

That Marriage Bed of Procrustes

In New Orleans during the war there wasn't any day and night, Sunday and weekday, what with the shipyards and war plants working three shifts all the time, and when such winter as there was began to break up, there wasn't any Mardi Gras. It was cancelled because of shortages and restrictions.

The Mardi Gras was one of the two things—the French Quarter was the other—that had brought George and Alice Fuller to New Orleans of all the places there were jobs in those days, but after being vaguely disappointed by the cancellation, the Fullers didn't give it another thought. They were too busy. They were also too busy to get any pleasure out of living in the Quarter. They worked every day for months on end, and they worked different shifts so that they had to force their whole life together into the few hours between the time Alice got home from work and George left, say between 4:30 and 10:30.

During this interlude, once, they lay silently smoking, each withdrawn to an outside edge of their enormous bed—actually the bed wasn't a bed at all but two small beds that could be pushed together against an enormous headboard and faked up to look like an enormous bed. However their recent exertions had worked the beds apart and there was now a wide gap between them.

Alice was crying—probably she was crying, anyway—she always did. George listened carefully to her breathing. Yes, she was crying. "It's no use," she said. Her voice was low but steady.

She might be right, he thought. It probably was no use. But what the hell? What happened after you admitted it was no use? What then?

"It's just no use," she said.

She was being quiet anyway. That helped a lot. He wanted to say something comforting, but there wasn't much to say. Since she wasn't screaming that it was his fault, he wanted to go part way at least toward admitting that it might be his fault. But he didn't say anything. He got up on his elbow. His bed creaked faintly.

"Just no damn use," she said.

He knew he had to say something. Still he was glad he hadn't admitted any fault. She wouldn't forget it. She'd use it next time— because there would be a next time no matter what she said or he thought—and she'd never forget it. That was her way. Anything he might say would be taken in and burned in her brain and blasted out at him hotter than anything Bessemer ever dreamed of. Every answer, all logic, pride, humility, love, hate—whatever he gave would come back to sear him. She'd use it forever and never let him forget what he said, and for the rest of his life he would pay for that weak moment of honesty.

And he didn't say anything because he knew there was nothing to say, but just the same he opened his mouth.

"No use at all," she said.

He was going to say something. "I was twelve years old," he said and stopped. She couldn't have been more surprised than he was.

"Oh, Jesus," she said. "You still are." But she said it quietly.

He bit his lip because he shouldn't have given her that opening:

he knew the rules by now. "One day when I was twelve," he said—at least he was talking. Even if he wasn't saying what he wanted to say or what needed to be said, at least he was making words between them.

"What's the use?" she said.

"There was this calendar," he said, closing his ears and even his eyes, closing himself up tight and reaching across the gulf between the beds with only his voice.

"What's the use of all this?" Alice said.

"I don't know," he said. "Maybe no use. I can't tell until later."

"Fumble, fumble," Alice said. "Everything you do, fumbling around."

There was no answer to that that wouldn't have given her a chance to enlarge painfully on the subject, so he just went ahead. "There was this picture on the calendar in the barber shop back home. I can remember all about the shop, but what I want to tell you about is this picture of this woman."

"This I have to hear," Alice said. She had lighted another cigarette and now she flopped over on her back, puffing angrily at the ceiling, the fingers of one hand tapping sharply against the headboard.

"The picture was a girlie picture, exactly what you would expect to find in an old time shop like Frank Lavalle's. Only then I didn't know that there was anything like it in all the world.

"Now that I think back on it Frank must have been rather wonderful. He still wore long sweeping mustaches like the men in old pictures, and he kept the sleeves of his shirt tucked up with jazz garters. His hair was thick and white, and his face was very red. He must have been older than God even then. He claimed he had been a barber sixty years on the same spot.

"This time I'm talking about, Frank looked up as I came in—when I think back over it, I see myself standing in the doorway and he is looking over his left shoulder at me. He nodded to me but went on talking with the man in the chair. The only other customer

ahead of me was Mr. Barker, who sometimes left his haberdashery
and came down for a shave about this time of day. I sat down and
took a look around the shop.

"I knew exactly what there was to see. Directly opposite me
there was a fine large calendar with a picture of a bear showing its
cubs how to catch fish. I still see that picture once in a while in
garages and country stores.

"All I had to do was sit there facing the bears and just move
my eyes a little and I could see this picture of this woman. So I sat
there facing the bears, but my eyes seemed to be shooting out dotted
lines right to the other picture—remember the way Hairbreadth
Harry's eyes would shoot out dotted lines and fix Rudolph Rassen-
dale to the spot in the funny papers?"

"We never had Hairbreadth Harry in our paper," Alice said,
punching her pillow into shape against the headboard.

He felt as if he had had the wind knocked out of him, and he
rested a moment. He had asked for it—he had to admit that—but
still it would be nice just once not to get it when he asked for it.
He began again cautiously because he knew he was getting onto
dangerous ground.

"Anyway, as beautiful and all as the woman was, I couldn't
quite see anything. Perhaps if I turned my head or took another
chair or walked right up to the picture. But I didn't dare do any
of those things although I seemed to be right on the verge of dis-
covering something wonderful. God knows what."

He held his breath, inwardly cursing his carelessness, but she
was silent. "Are you asleep?" he said softly.

"No," she said. "I just couldn't make up my mind which of a
dozen things to say first."

"Frank shook out the cloth with a loud snap. The man in the
chair got up. He was a farmerish looking man and he fumbled a
long time in his overalls pocket for the money. Mr. Barker took off
his coat and loosened his vest and tie and sat back in the chair.

Frank began to lather him up. I got up and walked over to the pile of magazines. They were *Film Fun*'s and *Judge*'s and *Whizbang*'s. It was my subtle intention to select a magazine and then go sit in another chair as if by chance so I could have a better look at the woman in the calendar.

"While I was standing there trying to pick out a magazine, the Hathaway baker came in and stood beside Frank, who was stropping his razor. The Hathaway baker was a person well worth listening to because he was supposed to know more stories than anyone else anywhere. Kids who had heard his stories said they were full of French women and Chinese women and farmer's daughters who were somehow different from the girls in my grade in school whose fathers were farmers and fairies who weren't fairies at all but something else very mysterious and awful.

"The Hathaway baker and Frank put their heads together and turned their backs on me. Mr. Barker lifted up his lathered face and listened. I listened too, but I couldn't hear anything that made any sense. That was quite a disappointment."

"I'll bet," Alice said. "I'll bet it was a disappointment. You got to get your kicks some way. I always said you were deaf though. Maybe that's your trouble. Maybe you're deaf. Maybe if you got a hearing aid you'd be better in bed."

He understood fully that it ought to have amused him to see her try so hard—he knew that she knew his hearing was excellent—but still he felt a flash of anger. He would have snapped at her, but he saw her watching him sharply as if wondering whether he realized she had spoken foolishly. That look of hers satisfied him, for he knew he couldn't possibly win more than that if he tried to argue.

"I was listening as hard as I could and watching. I could see the baker stroke his chin as if he had a beard, and then he puffed out his chest and pranced around the chair with one hand on the back of his head and the other hand on his hip the way men do when they imitate women. Mr. Barker laughed and slapped his thigh, and Frank smiled under his white mustache and stropped his razor faster and faster. At the end the baker gave a high squeaky laugh like a crazy man and ran out of the shop.

"I was so busy looking out the window and watching the baker get into his truck and arrange his basket with bread and cake and things that I walked right back to the same chair and sat down before I realized what I was doing. Embittered by my stupidity I stared directly at the woman in the calendar, but I could see only her shoulder and hip and most of all her eyes, which seemed to be looking over her shoulder directly at me. I couldn't make anything of that look. I knew there was something there but I didn't know what. That woman wasn't saying anything. She was just looking."

"Poor boy," Alice said. "Nobody ever tells him anything and he has to be told—even four letter words he has to be told."

Silence had worked so well for him last time, winning him that uncertain look, that he tried it again, but now she lay with her eyes fixed on the ceiling.

"I looked down at my magazine to hide from that woman's eyes. I had selected a *Whizbang* because *Film Fun* had nothing but girls in bathing suits and underwear and fur rugs and maybe a cowboy hat held up in front of them, and it was all a tease. Always those same shoulders, hips, and eyes. And always that same look that suggested there was much much more. But what? I had read through a magazine each time I came for a haircut, but no secret was ever revealed. I despaired of *Film Fun* and tried *Whizbang* for a change."

"Maybe you're blind," Alice said, still not looking at him.

"*Whizbang* was pretty much the same except that there was one cartoon I understood right off. This was a picture of a fellow sitting at a lunch counter, and there was a waitress leaning over to take his order. She had on a low cut dress. A counter man in the back was yelling, 'Hold the grapefruit.' Some joke. Even then I didn't think it was funny. But I continued to stare at the page because if there was one thing I knew, it was what a breast should look like. This miserable scrawl made the bulging breasts as hard as stone cannon balls, but I saw only warm and living flesh.

"It doesn't really matter whether it was good or bad art: I was ready for it. And I was ready for it because Miss Ross the music teacher wore low cut dresses. She'd come around and put her head down close so she could listen while all the class sang. Her long hair fell down and tickled your face. The front of her dress swung open. And there they were. Warm, soft, delicately curved, gently swaying. And then I had to sit on my hands because—well, I just about had to touch them or die. I didn't know why: the woman in the calendar wouldn't tell me, *Film Fun* wouldn't tell me, and try as I would I couldn't hear enough from the Hathaway baker or Frank.

"I sat there staring at the cartoon, visualizing Miss Ross in the position of the waitress because that was the only position I was capable of visualizing her in."

"I'll have to remember that position," Alice said. "It doesn't sound like much, but anything is worth a try."

"What I mean to say is that time passed like lightning. I was lost in a wonderful maze of exotically pendulous breasts—all of them nippleless, of course, because Miss Ross' dresses weren't cut that low."

"Say," she said, "when did you learn about nipples? I didn't know you knew about nipples."

"Oh, for god's sake shut up," he shouted.

"That's right," she said. "Get mad. Shout. That helps a lot. Why don't you hit me? Maybe you'd like that. Maybe we can get a little whip if you like it."

"You are my whip, dearest," he said.

"You bastard. You lousy bastard. You crown of thorns. You four sharp nails. You gall. You wormwood. You big spear in my side."

"Oh, Jesus," he said. It was no use. One word from him always hit the jackpot and he got a thousand back. He determined to give up the story but he discovered he couldn't give it up.

"I mean, Mr. Barker got out of the chair and paid Frank. I put the magazine down and stepped forward."

"Do you have to go on telling this stupid story?" Alice said.

"I guess I do," George said, "the same way you have to go on being a bitch."

"You blind deaf twelve-year-old bastard. You fetus in the dark." She pronounced each word distinctly and slowly as if they were stones and she was throwing them viciously but with great care.

George silently hunched himself into the storm. Then when she was through he began his story again.

"Anyway, Frank said, 'Read any good jokes?'

"'Hold the grapefruit,' I said because it was the only thing I could think of.

"'Heh, heh.' Frank's mustache shook. 'Hear that, Robert?' He held his cupped hands out in front of him as if he were weighing two small packages of approximately equal weight. He and Mr. Barker laughed, and I laughed too although I didn't know what they were laughing about, but it seemed to have something to do with what I said. Mr. Barker heaved himself into his coat and left chuckling.

"Frank took a razor in his hand and came around in front of me. 'Shave?' he said, peering into my face. I shook my head because I couldn't think of anything to say. I squirmed in the chair as he leaned over me with the razor. 'It won't be long now,' he said and smiled, and I knew he was only making some sort of fun of me, and I shook my head again. I was spared any more of his humor because just then we heard Joe Murphy's team of bays passing in the street. Frank put down the razor and stood at the window watching. He had completely forgotten about me, and I was just as glad.

"I watched the horses over Frank's shoulder. I saw the near horse lift its tail. Then Frank distracted me from the horses. No sooner had the horse lifted its tail than Frank left the window and ran to the closet and got out his little shovel and bucket and ran out into the street. He used to have a garden out back and he was always on the look out for free fertilizer.

"I could see Frank squatting in the middle of the street while the cars whizzed by him on either side. Some of the drivers stared at him and some made remarks I couldn't hear. I glanced at the clock and saw that I had only half an hour to get up to church—we were being prepared for confirmation just then. I began to fidget and thought for the first time that I could understand why some people objected to Frank's running out of the shop to gather manure, but on the other hand those were the same people who objected to his eating pie while he was cutting hair, and that didn't seem to slow him up any."

"He couldn't eat pie and cut hair at the same time," Alice said. "Barbers always use both hands."

"I can remember going home and combing the crumbs out of my hair," George said.

"In the mirror I watched Frank come back into the shop and wash his hands briskly in the basin the way doctors do in movies. 'Just what my garden needs,' he said snipping his shears in anticipation.

" 'Please, Mr. Lavalle,' I said, 'I have to get up to church by nine o'clock.'

" 'I'll have you out in plenty of time,' Frank said. 'Going to have a ball game in the church with them graven images?' (This was because I had my glove with me in case we had time for a game after instruction.) He seemed to enjoy the idea. He chuckled over it but then put it away with the resolute air of a man who knows how to give serious things their due.

" 'Anyways,' Frank said, 'a game's a good thing.' He leaned around and nodded over my shoulder. 'Exercise is a good thing.

Keeps you regular. I always exercise. Regular as a clock. In the summertime I work in the garden. I was up this morning and worked two hours in the garden. And in the winter if I feel I'm getting unregular, do I take a laxative? No, sir. I saw wood. Better than any laxative going, I tell you.' He swung me around and told me, looking me straight in the eye until I flinched. He straightened my head firmly, but I kept my eyes lowered. This, then, was the barbershop.

"A whole battery of barber jokes fell into place for the first time. A whole area of reserve on the part of my mother about Frank Lavalle and his shop began to open up before me. I had penetrated into the inner mystery of the barber shop, the essence that explained everything: in the barber shop they talk about going to the bathroom as freely as one ordinarily does about going to a movie."

"Maybe you had the wrong toilet training," Alice said. "I'll have to ask your mother."

Thinking that she never let anything go, he let it go. It made him feel magnanimous, the filthy bitch.

"Well, how it was at home with my mother—not about toilet training, by the way, but strictly related topics—well, it was hard for her after my father died, you know."

"No, I don't know," Alice said, making it as hard as possible.

"Well, with a son to bring up and all," George said, shouldering his penance. "Take this night that must have been just a little before this haircut. It was bed time. I had just put out the light and got into bed when I heard my mother pause in front of the door. I braced myself in the dark, and as soon as I heard her gentle tap on the door, I felt the heat begin to rise in my face. 'Are you in bed?' my mother said softly.

" 'Yes,' I said.

" 'May I come in?' she said.

" 'Yes,' I said.

"She came and sat on the very edge of the bed while I lay still, very hot and uncomfortable. 'How have you been feeling lately?' she said.

" 'Fine,' I said.

" 'I thought at supper that your tongue looked a little coated,' she said, 'and when you spoke just now, your breath didn't smell quite right.' There was enough light for me to see that her face was turned away from me.

" 'I forgot to brush my teeth,' I said. That was a direct lie, but, hoping to avert the painful crisis of the moment, I was willing to go even that far.

"My mother, however, having forced herself to this point, was unwilling to waste all she had endured. 'Are you sure you don't need a physic?' she said.

" 'No, I don't need one,' I said.

" 'Well, if you do, let me know.' She got up, kissed me lightly, and left hurriedly. When I heard her settle in the living room, I went to the bathroom and made a lot of noise brushing my teeth. In the mirror my face didn't seem unduly red, but it still felt decidedly warm.

"Maybe that helps explain why when someone looked me in the face and talked about bowels, I felt I had really been let into a mystery. It seems inconceivable that I could ever have been so ignorant—or rather let me say innocent because that was the moment I stopped being innocent and began to be ignorant."

Alice snorted.

"I began to be ignorant," he repeated. "I said it again for you without your even asking."

"Thanks a lot," Alice said.

"Sometimes I think that all I have ever learned since has only contributed to my ignorance. But when Frank first began talking about regularity, I had no idea what he meant except I thought vaguely it had something to do with being at work every day. But when Frank said *laxative* the whole thing crashed open like Ali Baba's cave when he said *sesame*. I kept my eyes lowered but I felt that even the tips of my ears must give away my inner turmoil: horror, shame, fascination.

"Still, after the first triumph of being admitted into the mystery, I felt let down. (I don't know whether I got off to a bad start here in my conditioning or if it is in the nature of mysteries, but I have never since entered a mystery that didn't disappoint me.) Was this all there was? There simply had to be more. I would have to wait and listen as before. Only now I could be knowing about the bowels and pretend I knew more than I actually did, and so learn more and more all the time.

" 'I'm very regular,' I forced myself to say without looking up.

"But Frank seemed to have exhausted the bowels as a topic of conversation and went on snip snipping.

"The last few tufts of hair rolled down the white cloth over my hands and onto the floor. Frank spun the chair around facing the mirror. He held up a little mirror behind my head. 'How's that?' he said.

"I raised my eyes but I didn't seem to be able to focus on the back of my head. I saw the double-barreled bottles against the big mirror and Frank's face looking over my shoulder trying to catch my eye in the mirror. 'Fine,' I said. 'It looks fine.'

"Frank whipped the cloth off and I stepped down, feeling in my watch pocket for the quarter and the dime I had put there for the haircut. By the time I got the money out, Frank, who had held out his hand when I began fumbling, had pivoted around his hand so that he was standing before the window. His hand, however, remained exactly in place. His fist closed over the money. He didn't look at me or the money as he said, 'Just look at that.' So I looked out the window but all I saw was a girl from my grade in school, Mary Duane. She was wearing shorts and a tee shirt and eating an ice cream cone. 'There's something nice for a boy like you,' Frank said. I shook my head and smiled—or it may have been a grimace. 'Go on,' Frank said. He poked me in the ribs with his hair brush.

I laughed a funny little laugh that I had never laughed before: I didn't know what Frank was talking about, so it didn't seem really funny.

"'Hear that, George?' Frank said to George Holland, who was just then coming into the shop for his regular shave. He was the only man in town then to get a shave every day. 'He didn't admit it but he didn't deny it.' They both laughed hard at that.

"'He'll do all right if he can keep a secret,' George Holland said.

"'How about that?' Frank said.

"I laughed the same little laugh and picked up my glove and went out. I could hear them still laughing in the shop.

"Out in the street I tried the laugh again but I couldn't get it right."

"And you never got it right again," his wife said.

He heard her but it didn't matter any more. "That's right," he said.

"Anyway, I kept trying—"

"Oh, you keep trying," she said. "Try, try again with me dying inside piece after piece. Why don't you laugh? I made a joke, just the kind of joke you love, you filthy-minded snot." She burlesqued a laugh herself. "Ha, ha, ha, and ha," she said bitterly.

"I kept trying because if it was so funny I wanted to be able to use it again. I thought that perhaps that laugh would lead someone to say something further sometime at the barber shop. I thought I was on the threshold of something tremendous. I might learn about the woman in the calendar and about Mary Duane too—even she seemed to be part of it. And it may be that it was my unconscious resentment of her being part of it that led me that year to bedevil her by jabbing her with pens and pencils until the teacher changed our seats although we had always been good friends—and still were within certain limits and with some reservations."

"Pens and pencils," Alice said. "How obvious can you get?"

"Oh, for god's sake, I know that as well as you do now," he said. "You got all your Freud from me in the first place."

"And you got it all from a book," she said, having as usual the last and unanswerable word. And she added, just for good measure, "Remind me to bring my pencil box to bed next time. Something's got to work." She laughed again, not unpleasantly this time, and propped herself against the headboard. The headboard shook and the vibrations made his bed rock until he thought he would be seasick. But in spite of that he found himself responding to her softer mood, and he despised himself for it.

"Once I got outside the shop I remembered that it was very late, and I began to run as fast as I could because it was no joke if Father Sullivan caught you coming in late. Why, on Sunday he would even stop Mass and turn—"

"My god," Alice said, "isn't this story over yet?"

He had been prepared to go on indefinitely, but suddenly it seemed to him that whatever it was he had to say was either said by now or never would be. He was tired. Alice was standing beside her bed. She shook a sheer nightgown down over her nakedness.

"Will you get up and let me straighten the beds?" she said. "Or even help me if that's not asking too much. Even a twelve-year-old can be expected to help with the beds." She was no longer interested in what she was saying, but was saying it more or less automatically. He got up and they pushed the two beds together. She smoothed the sheets and arranged her pillows for reading.

He slipped into his clothes hurriedly before she was even aware what he was doing. "Why, where are you going?" she said, sitting up in bed, her book on her lap not yet opened.

"Out," he said.

"When will you be back?" she said.

"Who says I'll be back?" He went out enjoying to the fullest the look of surprise on her face. He had never said anything like that before. In fact that was one of the things he was conscious every time that he might say and very carefully avoided saying, things hoarded up for a devastating effect some time when he didn't care how he hurt her: things like her father's suicide when the market broke in '29, like her documented inability to have children, like the failure of her first marriage.

"Are you going looking for Mary Duane?" she called after him. "Mary Duane," she repeated slowly as if hefting a new weapon. He didn't answer.

Now he had expended one of the best things in his armory. Too bad, if he wasn't going back, that he hadn't used them all up in one great broadside. He went along the gallery and down the stairs into the patio where the rustle of dried leaves sounded like the ghost of water splashing in the dusty, debris-clogged fountain.

Once he was out of the house he walked a block toward Canal Street and then a block toward the river and then half a block away from Canal Street. Then he crossed the street and walked back on the other side toward Canal Street although he was going to Canal Street only because he could follow it to the one place where he could see the river, the hidden river that everywhere else he could only guess at as it sailed along over his head just a little way off.

And then he stopped. He didn't want to go to the river after all. The river at New Orleans is wrong. If George hadn't known that, the river would have been just what he needed. To face the river and feel it. To feel it run from right to left in front of him. To think: this way to the sea. This way up into the continent. This is south. That is north. In front is west. Behind is east. To be face to face with a great and obviously incontrovertible fact and to become oriented in the security of that fact.

But the river is wrong. At the foot of Canal Street where the traveler from the east at last runs into the river, the river is running momentarily north. And even knowing this did him no good. To look at the river, which should represent certainty, to see in his mind's eye from earliest childhood that great black line running true from north to south from top to bottom of his map, from Great Lakes to great Gulf, and to have to remind himself that now it was running north outraged any world he had ever had or ever hoped to have. The first time he saw the river he felt enormously satisfied. The river was something to begin with. It was a base line. Then when he discovered that although the river inevitably flowed toward the Gulf yet at the only point at which he could see it it flowed north, a demand was made upon him and upon his faith that he couldn't answer. There was his river. There always in his mind's eye was his map. In the end he could trust neither.

He stood still on the sidewalk in the old part of town, alone and undecided. Then he wasn't alone. The door of a courtyard near at hand opened and out came, first, a very small clown with mask and horn and noisemaker, and then, a mammy-type colored woman. They came toward George and he began automatically to walk toward them.

When they met, the clown blew his horn and shook his noisemaker at George. The clown stood and watched George, quick dark eyes through the mask. George stood and watched the clown. The mammy said, "You really were frightened, weren't you, sir?"

"Terribly," George said. "Yes, terribly frightened."

"You see?" the mammy said to the clown. But the clown said nothing.

"I was so frightened I couldn't even scream," George said. "I couldn't run or anything."

"You see?" the mammy said. The clown decided to laugh. He shrieked laughter and he danced. And now George stood truly immobilized. He had forgotten such delight. It had disappeared so completely from his world that he had forgotten it was even possible. The clown shook his noisemaker again but was unable to compose himself for blowing his horn.

"He gets Mardi Gras mixed up with Halloween," the mammy said.

"Why, it is Mardi Gras time, isn't it?" George said.

"You wouldn't think so with no parades. It's more like Lent already," the mammy said. "All right," she said to the clown, "now you've frightened someone, home you go." The clown turned promptly and went back through the gate into the courtyard. "Thank you, sir, for being frightened," the mammy said.

George stood outside the gate. Over the wall he could hear the noisemaker constantly, a laugh, the thin faraway sound of the horn, another laugh, sheer delight, and the closing of a further door.

And then he went home.